TARAN

A Time Travel Romance

JANE STAIN

ISBN: 9781 9806 11615

Foreword

Battle of Harlaw

by Sir Walter Scott
 (1771–1832)

Now hald your tongue, baith wife and carle (peasant),
 And listen, great and small,
 And I will sing of Glenallan's Earl
 That fought on the red Harlaw.

The [loud shout]'s cried on Bennachie,
 And doun the Don and all,
 And highland and lowland may mournful be
 For the [severe] field of Harlaw.

They saddled a hundred milk-white steeds,

They bridled a hundred black,
With a [chevron] of steel on each horse's head,
And a good knight upon his back.

They hadna ridden a mile, a mile,
A mile, but barely ten,
When Donald came branking (strutting) down the brae
With twenty thousand men.

Their tartans they were waving wide,
Their [gloves] were glancing clear,
The [bagpipes] rung frae side to side,
Would deafen ye to hear.

The great Earl in his stirrups stood,
That Highland host to see;
'Now here a knight that's stout and good
May prove a jeopardy.

'What would'st thou do, my squire so gay,
That rides beside my rein,
Were ye Glenallan's Earl the day,
And I were Roland Cheyne?

'To turn the rein were sin and shame,
To fight were wondrous peril;
What would ye do now, Roland Cheyne,
Were ye Glenallan's Earl?'

'Were I Glenallan's Earl this tide,
And ye were Roland Cheyne,
The spur should be in my horse's side,
And the bridle upon his mane.

'If they hae twenty thousand blades,
And we twice ten times ten,
Yet they hae but their tartan plaids,
And we are mail-clad men,

'My horse shall ride through ranks sae rude,
As through the moorland fern -
Then ne'er let the gentle Norman blood
Grow cauld for Highland kerne (rabble).'

Photo: WolfatDunkeld

The Wolf of Badenoch's tomb at the Cathedral of Dunkeld in Perthshire is one of the few Scottish royal monuments to have survived from the Middle Ages.

The Wolf was the third surviving son of King Robert II of Scotland. In English his name was Alexander Stewart, but in Gaelic it was Alasdair Mór mac an Rígh. He was Earl of Buchan, and he lived from 1343 to 1405.

Photo taken by Gil Campbell and put into the public domain as an upload on Your UK.

Chapter One

Lauren tried to shrink down into the floor and disappear while Senga bustled about, sweeping ash from the hearth and checking on Lauren's progress with the breakfast dishes. As soon as Senga left the manor's kitchen, Taran was going to ask Lauren difficult questions. Perhaps she had better use these few minutes of respite to gauge Taran's face. Did he look angry?

No, not angry. Worse. Taran's devilishly handsome face was deeply suspicious and... and his feelings were hurt.

Lauren couldn't say she blamed him. This was one heck of a secret she was keeping.

"Galdus!" she asked inside her head, silently. "Galdus, why did ye na keep me from saying those things aloud?"

All she got out of Galdus in reply was his gleeful

cackle. It rattled around inside her mind like the echo of a coin falling on a tiled floor. He had never refused to answer her before, not in the whole three months since Deirdre had given her the dagger, back in the time of the druids.

She tried again. "Galdus?"

Nothing.

Lauren jumped a bit, realizing she'd been stroking the dagger that hung at her hip. The ghost of Galdus, an ancient druid, lived on inside the dagger. Still furious at him, she pulled her hand away as if she'd been burned, then made a point of grabbing another dirty tankard to wash.

Oh no.

Senga nodded approvingly at Lauren and was leaving the kitchen, which meant that in just a few moments, Lauren and Taran would be alone. How much had he heard? How much trouble was she in? And why on earth had Galdus goaded her into saying all that out loud? Especially when he'd been blocking her from explaining the same things to Jessica and Katherine for months?

The time for wondering was gone, and the time for reckoning had begun. The kitchen door closed with a swish, leaving her alone with Taran in the windowless stone kitchen his parents had built as a protection cell, highly unusual.

Lauren was done with the dishes and searched around for something else to do. The kitchen fire was blazing merrily. Senga was no slouch. There weren't even any pots to stir, because most of them would eat their noon meal at Gus's tavern in town, after the wash was done and before the militia mustered for practice.

She couldn't meet Taran's eyes, just spoke to the wall.

"I dinna suppose there would be any point in asking ye how much ye heard."

He chuckled just the tiniest little bit and came over to stand a few feet away beside her, leaning back and putting his hands on the counter behind him.

"I heard enough tae ken ye hae a master someplace that ye speak tae by way o' magic, and that this master o' yers wishes tae send ye off intae the winter alone on a quest for what ye call an artifact."

She put her hands on the counter behind them as well, leaning back and mimicking his casual attitude — which she knew was an act. But it gave her hope. If he was trying to act casual, then he wasn't going to run off and tell everyone. At least not right away.

"What are ye thinking?" she asked, still not looking at him, afraid of what she would see in his face. Had it turned to anger yet?

"'Tis na sae far-fetched anymair, the three o' ye being from the future. Ye did hae those breather things. And ye are talking tae someone who is na here."

"I dinna want tae talk tae him," she said with as much earnestness as she could manage, considering her knees were trembling in dread of what he might say.

She had been starting to like Taran, and now this had to happen.

He slowly put out his hand with his palm up, the way Father Craig did when he spoke of logical progressions.

"Aye, that much I ken, some aught tae dae with the way ye were talking tae him."

A kernel of hope bloomed in Lauren's heart. Taran was having a sense of humor about this. And he still hadn't run off to tell his brother Leif, the Laird of Cresh Manor. He sure wasn't making this easy for her, though.

"Are na ye gaun'ae ask questions?" she said with that hope.

When he didn't say anything, she turned to look at him.

Big mistake.

He turned to look at her as well, and the way he raised his eyebrow as if to say 'are you kidding me?' made his eyes sparkle with intelligence and awareness. So much so that it was almost unbearable.

She had to rein herself in, or she would just stare at him. Drifting off into a stupor already, she took a deep breath and turned back to the dishes. The perfect excuse not to get drawn into his too perceptive gaze. She picked up the tankard she'd been washing.

"It would be much easier tae explain if ye asked questions, ye ken?"

Senga's voice preceded her back into the kitchen, making Lauren sigh with relief.

"Lauren, I can take over in the kitchen now. Why don't you go outside and enjoy the fresh air while ye help with the wash? 'Tis a braw day, as winter days gae."

With that, Senga bustled in, already raising her arms up in shooing motions. When she saw Taran was still in the kitchen, she put her hands on her hips.

"Why dae ye never help me with the dishes, eh?"

This made Lauren laugh despite her anxiety.

"We're going, Senga."

"Aye Senga, we're going," Taran called out as he hastily made an exit behind her.

They were alone in the great room now, and as they made their way to the back door to join the others at the washtub, Taran whispered in Lauren's ear. What he said might have been mistaken for romantic, if it weren't for the context. But her body responded to the feel of his breath near her ear anyway, even as she winced away to make sure he didn't touch her. His voice was soft, even sympathetic, but at the same time, he shared his older brother's air of command — not surprising, since they shared command of the town militia.

"Join me for a walk directly after supper. Dinna allow anyone tae come along."

Turning to look him in the eye just before they went out the back door, Lauren nodded her assent.

He nodded and even bowed a bit to her before turning and making his way down into the tiny village, which he called the town of Inverurie.

While helping fellow time travelers Amy and Katherine with the washing, Lauren leaned in and quietly asked Katherine, "Will ye take over my turn at the dishes tonight? Taran has asked me tae go for a walk with him after supper."

Katherine gave Lauren a high five, which Lauren guiltily accepted and returned.

"About time, girl. Go get him!"

Amy gave Lauren an encouraging wink and shrug. The older woman had arrived only a month ago, but she had glommed onto Jessica and Katherine when they were captives of the time-manipulating druids. Amy shared a bedroom now with Katherine and Lauren, so Lauren was friends with Amy too.

Dinner was pleasant enough. Lauren enjoyed a respite while visiting with Taran's brother Leif and Taran's sister-in-law, Jessica, Lauren's college room-mate, whom she and Galdus had brought here into the 1400s. Katherine had come with them, too. She was the top salesperson for their modern-day employer, PenUlt. Luag was at the table with them, Leif and Taran's friend from afar. Luag and Katherine never quit sniping at each other. At first it had been amusing, but three months later it was annoying, like listening to your brothers and sisters squabbling.

At long last, supper was done.

Lauren rose from the table with a grateful look at Katherine, who nodded with excitement, shaking her fists in front of her in glee. Lauren then turned toward her college roommate Jessica, now lady of Crest Manor.

"May I be excused, yer ladyship?"

Lauren didn't have to address Jessica this way, but she took great pleasure in doing so.

Visibly taking great pleasure in it as well, Jessica nodded.

"Aye, that ye may."

Jessica winked.

Lauren looked over at Katherine scoldingly.

Katherine shrugged and smiled.

Could no one keep their mouths shut in this house?

But Lauren found herself smiling back at her two friends, the grin of the cat who ate the canary. She couldn't resist watching Taran's Pictish nose, his knowing dark eyes, and his toned warrior's body as he took the pipe Senga handed him and gestured for Lauren to join him at the front door.

A pipe? She'd never seen Taran smoke before. Never mind.

He donned his leather cloak, held her shawl for her while she put it on, and opened the door. The two of them made their way out, but instead of starting on the long hike up the mountain behind Cresh Manor, Taran walked toward a small cottage. Lauren had never been inside. He produced a large key and fumbled with the lock.

"This has stood empty since Gammer died," he explained. "Leif kens I wished a word with ye, for I had tae ask him for the key."

She searched his face for any sign of antagonism, but it looked like he was just giving her a social warning.

"What dae ye suppose he thinks ye mean tae speak with me aboot?"

Taran shrugged as he got the door open, but as usual, he had that knowing glint in his eyes. It was mesmerizing. He turned and led her into a tiny one-room cottage with a bed, table and chairs, a tiny hearth, and not much more.

After gesturing for Lauren to take a seat at the tiny little table, Taran turned to some wood that had probably been sitting by the hearth for a decade, it was so dusty. She did notice that nothing else was dusty. Perhaps Leif let Senga in here to clean once in a while. Interesting.

Lauren couldn't help but love the little cottage, and she took this opportunity to admire the place while Taran built a fire and lit it with an ember he carried in the pipe.

Aha, that's why he brought the pipe.

Now that she took the time to look, she saw the tiny washstand in the corner, complete with a beautiful stoneware wash bowl and pitcher. The hearth stones were smooth river rocks, artfully arranged. The cottage held a featherbed still, a luxurious item that she, Katherine, and Amy could use in their room. What was it doing here, unused?

Great loving care was taken with this tiny cottage, and Lauren hated the idea of giving Taran bad memories of the place, but he seemed determined to get answers out of her.

"Well Galdus," Lauren said in her mind, "if ye're gaun'ae shut my mouth, pray tell me now. Save me the shame."

Galdus's eerie voice came into her mind for the first time that day.

"Ye hae learned the way o' talking with yer body, sae I dinna see the point in closing yer mouth. Na till I hae control o' yer body as wull. It will come, mark me." Galdus laughed that disturbing laugh of his.

Once the fire was burning merrily, warming the frigid room, Taran took the other seat at the tiny little table. Shivering now that they had been outside the warmth of the manor house awhile, they both moved their chairs closer to the fire.

Taran's handsome eyes looked at her expectantly. His face was more passive than she'd ever seen it. He was a man of action, so she knew she would only get one chance to explain before he made a decision and set upon a course.

She gave him her best cute girl look, scrunching up her face with a smile.

"Are ye sure ye willna ask me questions?"

He gave her a sad shake of his head.

"Lauren, this is na one o' yer games. Heed, I ken ye are unsettled by whatever ye plan tae tell me. I will hear ye out, but 'tis understanding each the other that is needed here. I am deciding what tae dae about ye. Sae hear my plea. Tell me all the truth, the whole o' it. Any bit o' the story may help me yet tae remain on friendly terms with ye."

His look was so sincere, so pleading, so painfully earnest, that she had to look away in shame. Why hadn't she just told everyone at the beginning, as soon as she arrived here? Katherine had already spilled the beans and told the household they were from the future...

Galdus's cackling laughter answered that question. He didn't want it known that he was gradually taking control of her. Truth to tell, she hadn't realized it herself when she first arrived here. Galdus's influence was that insidious.

Lauren peeked up at Taran through her long lashes.

He was sitting patiently, awaiting her answer. 'I'm giving ye a chance,' his eyes told her. 'Take it, lass.'

Sighing, she did.

"In my youth, I worked with a large troupe of historical re-enactors whenever they came to town—"

"What does that hae tae dae—"

"Please. Hear me out. Ye promised. Save yer questions for the end, aye?"

"Aye."

"The troupe was run by a small branch of the MacGregor clan. Years later, I found out they are really from the 1500s. Their family are slaves to the druids, who send them to fetch artifacts for them from different periods of time."

She rubbed her sweaty palms on her thick woolen leine, looking at the fire.

"The druids could go themselves, but that's problematic for longer trips. They either disappear off the face of the earth while they're gone, or if they return the instant they left, well... A person ages normally in whatever time they're in, so if they stay long in another time period, when they arrive back in their time they are older than they should be, causing friends and foes to ask awkward questions. So the druids only time travel for themselves on brief trips. For any errand that takes more than a day or two, they send their slaves."

She had to look Taran in the face at this point, to make sure he got it. Her faire friend Kelsey had glossed over this part initially, and Lauren had been utterly confused. It was crucial to understanding why the druids used their peculiar modus operandi.

Curiosity and surprise lit his face, and his attention was rapt.

Good. But she still couldn't look at him while she spoke, because any second, his face might turn unfriendly. Hence, she returned her gaze to the warm fire he had made, speaking quickly so he would hear as much of it as possible before deciding to ... Best not to think of that possibility.

"While I was at the faire, the MacGregor boys didna ken about the family curse. Their four parents wanted them tae hae good childhoods, and sae they only telt them about the curse once the eldest turned eighteen. There were six MacGregor boys, and they were courting six o' us lasses. One year, on Tavish and Tomas's birthday, they all parted company with us and disappeared with nary a trace. I was mystified about what happened till just last year, when one o' the lasses, Kelsey, telt me she was back together with Tavish. 'Tis a long story, but she unwittingly became a druid —"

"Aw, come now. How dae ye unwittingly become a druid?"

Lauren held up her hand and took a chance at glancing in Taran's face.

"Save yer questions for the end, remember?"

He nodded reluctantly, turning his head to the side and pressing his lips together.

This made her uneasy. Should she get up and leave?

She sighed. What was the point? She had already told him way too much to back down now. In fact, going on could only improve her case, so she persisted.

"Like I said, Kelsey unwittingly became a druid

and gained magical powers. Unfortunately, she didna get the power o' time travel. Nah, she got dream walking. She can talk tae me in my dreams nay matter where or when I am. She can with anyone she's ever touched. Anyway, through Tavish, she learned the whole story, and she telt the rest o' us lasses. And we all wanted tae travel through time."

She paused. Ostensibly, it was to catch her breath and warm her hands. But really, she wasn't proud of the next part of her tale. Oh, how naive and stupid she had been.

"I only got my hands on Galdus three months ago, just afore we came here. I got him in the foremaist century, from a Pictish lass named Deirdre — only Kelsey tells me she's na really a Pictish lass at all. She grew up at the castle near Port Patrick. Her mother marrit Laird Malcomb's nephew Alfred... Anyway, that's na really the point."

She might not get another chance, and so Lauren looked up into Taran's eyes.

They were still friendly, and she relaxed enough to notice he was biting his lip to prevent himself from speaking, but there was recognition in his eyes. He knew who Laird Malcomb had been...

No. Get to the point, Lauren. Quit beating around the bush.

"Anyhow," she said, placing her hand on the dagger, "eager I was, tae get my hands on Galdus. For I kenned he could travel through time. I was excited, and—"

Of its own volition, her hand reached up off the dagger and out toward Taran.

Lauren jumped up from her chair and ran across the room, pressing her back against the far wall.

"Rot in Hell, Galdus!" she raged in her mind.

After taking a moment to compose herself, she looked at the dagger significantly, then at Taran.

"The moment I touched Galdus, he spoke inside my mind. And he could hear me when I thought at him. Sometimes when I'm not even thinking straight at him, he responds to my thoughts —"

She broke off because of the screams she could hear, outside in the distance.

Chapter Two

Taran pushed open the door to his gammer's old cottage and gasped. The black night sky was like day below, because of the huge fire that blazed in town. The silo. All the grain they had was burning, and winter was only half over. Someone was going to pay.

Taran let out his war cry and ran into the manor for his sword and armor. He could see Leif and Luag already armored up with their swords, running down the trail through the barley fields.

Senga called out from behind the closed door of the kitchen.

"Go and get them, Taran. We lasses are safe. I hae them all with me, and I bolted the door."

"Well done."

He finished strapping on the leather pieces meant to protect him in battle: a vest, bracers, the hood. Over all this, he strapped on his sword, then ran out into the frigid night without his leather cloak. It would hinder him in a fight.

Just as he was turning to follow Luag and Leif, he saw Lauren running to join him. Not slowing down, he spoke to her out of the side of his mouth as they ran through the barley, where she caught up to him.

"I ken ye made short work o' that druid with... Galdus, Lauren. Howsoever, dae ye think ye are up tae the challenge o' facing whoever lies in wait below? 'Twill be out in the open. Ye willna hae a narrow door tae keep them coming at ye one at a time."

"I'm na up to it," she said as they ran, not having any trouble breathing, "but I hear tell there is none who can beat Galdus."

They were nearing the silo now, so fast were they running. She was keeping up with him step for step.

"If the way ye can run with him is any indication, then ye may hae the right o' it."

"Aye," she said as they entered the heat of the raging silo fire. "'Tis the way he woos his slaves. Makes himself sae useful, ye dinna want tae be withoot him. It gets tae the point where ye're sleeping with him, where yer never far enough away tae escape."

She slept with the dagger? His mind filled with dozens of questions.

But the fire pushed them all out.

Taran searched the surrounding area. The militia

must be engaging whoever had done this. Where was the fight?

He saw and heard nothing but the shouts of people, the crackling of the fire, and steam rising whenever someone tossed water on the blaze.

There was no one to fight. They had gotten away.

"Let's join the bucket line," Lauren suggested quietly. She gestured where town folk were relaying buckets full of water up from the river and empty buckets back down. It wasn't happening fast enough. The fire was winning.

Nodding, he ran over, craning his neck to watch the blaze for flying embers and ducking whenever some neared.

At first, he was hurt to see her join the line far away from him, but then he realized why. It wouldn't harm anything if she touched Alvin or Mauve. It didn't matter if her druid dagger heard their thoughts.

Leif was directing the people.

"Aiden, switch off with Jared being the one tae throw the water. Jared, take a turn throwing the water. Well done, all o' ye. That's the way. Keep the water coming. Faster."

Taran admired his brother's quick thinking. Aiden must be unbearably hot near the flames. The man needed longer breaks between his approaches, and Leif's directions were speeding up the water noticeably.

There was a loud crashing sound.

Leif grabbed hold of Aiden and the others who were close and ran.

Part of the support gave way, and the next thing Taran knew, the silo was falling like a chopped tree. It landed just where the people had been.

Everyone crossed themselves at having so narrowly missed their deaths.

"Good," Leif called out, "it fell toward the river and na on Muillear and Devany's new house!"

That got some feeble laughs, but more importantly, it broke the people out of their shock. They went back to work. It was more difficult now, because the fire was more spread out.

After a little while, a cheer went up, and Taran turned to see Jacob, the cooper, running out with his family, all of them carrying as many buckets as they could. Soon, the town was overcoming the fire. They had it out before it could spread.

Aiden was near the front of the line, and Taran approached.

"How did it start?"

"'Twas the oddest thing. Flames came from Alvin's hill like stars falling from the sky, three of them at once, and landed solidly on the silo."

Taran looked off in the direction Aiden was pointing. His heart sank, for what lay that way? The druid castle. He looked back at the charred remains of the silo. Another worry was they wouldn't have enough grain stores to finish out the winter. Now all that remained was what each family had in their pantry.

Knowing he and Leif had more than they could use, Taran turned and met his brother's eyes, showing some of the grief he felt for the people.

Leif nodded that he did plan to do something about it. His brother was a good man. He shouldn't have doubted Leif would do right by the people.

When every last ember was out, when smoke no longer rose and steam no longer hissed, Leif addressed everyone in the pitch-black night.

"On the morrow we will distribute our stores sae that every person has enough for the rest o' the winter—"

"Ye dinna hae tae do that, Leif."

"We wull get by."

"Aye, we are tough, ye ken?"

Leif smiled, and Taran knew it was because the people were so stubbornly prideful, they wouldn't even accept help in such a dire situation is this.

"In any case, now is the time tae go home and sleep, but latch yer shutters and yer doors, aye?"

"Aye."

"Ye hae the right o' that."

"'Twas unnatural, the way the fire came at the silo."

"Aye, first they make us sick, and now they take oor food. What did we ever dae tae them?"

The people grumbled, but they made their way back to their homes. Once everyone was inside with the doors closed and the windows shuttered, Leif, Taran, Lauren, and Luag made their way back through the barren winter barley fields and up the trail through the woods to Cresh Manor, where they could see their entire valley below them.

Little Amena called out from inside the kitchen as soon as they entered the house.

"Leif? Taran? Is it ye?"

"Aye," Leif called out to her in a soothing voice. "Ye lasses can come oot now, Senga."

There was a rattling as the old cook unbolted the door and opened it, and then Amena ran first into Taran's arms, and then into Leif's. Ever since their parents died six months ago, she'd treated them more like uncles than brothers. There was a big age difference. This was only the wee lass's seventh winter.

Leif's wife, Jessica, came out next, a practical and kindly lass, followed by her and Lauren's friend Katherine, 'Katherine the Beautiful' was how Taran thought of her. She was golden haired and lithe of limb. Her eyes were all for Luag, who called her out.

"See anything ye fancy?"

She bit her lip so as not to give him the satisfaction of laughing at his jest, but her eyes were haunted, serious.

"When ye were gone sae long, I... Anyway, 'tis glad we are ye came home."

Lauren met Taran's eyes.

He knew what she was thinking. They hadn't finished their talk. He gently shook his head nay and looked upstairs.

She nodded with relief, heading for the room she shared with Katherine and Amy.

Leif put his arm around Jessica and they walked upstairs together, closely followed by Luag, Amy, and Katherine.

As was part of the new ritual Taran was afraid wouldn't last much longer, he carried Amena upstairs to tuck her into bed before retiring to his own room.

Chapter Three

Lauren made small talk with Katherine and Amy before they fell asleep, but her heart wasn't in it. Was Taran telling Leif her secret even now? Would someone barge through the bedroom door and try to wrest Galdus from her? She kept the old rune-encrusted and jagged dagger close while she slept, guarding against just this possibility.

She had to be careful, but she was in control. Galdus wanted her to touch Taran so that Galdus could read Taran's thoughts. Galdus was a pain in the butt, but he was her ticket home, so she would just have to keep her distance from Taran.

She sighed and turned over. Jessica had Leif now, and Katherine was closer than she knew to getting Luag. You could tell just by the way they looked at each other, and it was funny they didn't realize it.

Everyone thought so. And here she was, dying to be with Taran the same way Jessica was with Leif...

Galdus chuckled wickedly in Lauren's mind while she lectured herself there.

No. Those knowing eyes and that smug smile are off-limits. Remember, Galdus mustn't have access to Taran's mind.

But admonishing herself didn't stop her from dreaming about Taran.

When she awoke, dread gripped her afresh. Would she go down to breakfast and find everyone staring at her uneasily? Well, she wasn't going to be the last one down, that was for sure. She jumped up, dressed and tidied herself, then breezed down the stairs.

The men were already at the table, speaking in low tones, but no one looked at her suspiciously or anything as she passed by on her way to the kitchen to see if Senga wanted help.

When Lauren brought the parritch out and sat down at her place, Taran looked at her significantly and signaled that they would continue their talk after they finished eating.

Great. She had told him all she really wanted to tell him. However, it meant more time alone with him, and her heart thrilled a bit despite herself.

At last they were finished eating.

Taran was more obvious this time, standing from the table and extending a hand toward her.

"Come oot on a walk with me, Lauren."

Even through her dread, Lauren smiled big at Jessica.

"May I be excused, yer ladyship?"

Jessica took visible pleasure in her new ladyhood as well. "Ye may," she said, nodding her head to the side formally. But the big grin on her face said, 'You get another chance with Taran!'

This time, Taran took Lauren on an actual walk, on the trail that defined the outskirt of the town, around the dormant snow-covered barley fields, the town's inner skirt.

When they were out of earshot, Lauren spoke without thinking, saying exactly what was on her mind. As soon as the words were out of her mouth, she knew the men of this time would think them inappropriate, coming from the mouth of a woman, and she cringed a tiny bit.

"What were ye men speaking o'?"

But Taran busted up laughing and looked at her askance, and his handsome grin showed he admired her assertiveness.

"Ye dinna beat around the bush, dae ye lass?"

She shook her head.

"Nay, and I willna allow ye tae change the subject, either."

She raised her chin and eyebrows expectantly.

He turned back to the trail.

"Nay, I didna expect ye would. There's talk in town o' storming the druid castle. Everyone's upset about the silo being burned o' course, but ye ken we canna go storm the castle. We were talking about what tae hae the men dae instead, tae get their minds off that and convince them they are doing some aught. We spoke o' building fences, digging ditches... ye ken, all the usual fortifications a town can muster."

She took a deep breath and let it out, looking at the snowy hills as she walked beside him.

"So then, ye didna tell them about my trouble with Galdus?"

He followed her gaze and spoke softly.

"Nay, I didna."

There was ice in the path where a small creek came down from the mountain. It had frozen around the stepping stones, which were slick with re-frozen snow.

Lauren looked at Taran.

He shrugged and turned around to head back toward Cresh Manor.

She shrugged and followed.

The wind was now at their backs, and it blew her hair into her face.

She undid the brooch that held her huge plaid shawl around her shoulders so she could pull a small part of it up over her head like a hood, then pinned it tightly down again so as not to let the cold winter wind get to her.

"Promise me ye will let me be the one tae tell them, aye?"

"Aye. Howsoever, ye dae need tae tell them soon."

"I ken that would be the best course," was all she was willing to say. She didn't want to lie.

He gave her a knowing look, and they walked the rest of the way back to the manor house, each of them lost in their thoughts. It was a comfortable silence full of half smiles and nods. It was strange but nice, being on a date with a man who kept his hands to himself. Smiling, she told herself she could get used to it. For Lauren had no doubt this was a date, per the mores of the time.

When the men went off to their regularly sched-uled fight practice in the town, Lauren waved goodbye to them. She spent the day helping Senga run the household, as did the rest of the women. Even Lady Jessica.

❧

AND SO IT WENT FOR SIX MONTHS.

They survived the winter, but they were all thin and sallow when winter became spring and the hunting was easier.

Galdus finally quit urging Lauren to leave, saying instead the coming conflict would take her where he needed her anyway.

The town planted their barley and oats.

Spring turned to summer. They gathered 1411's first harvest.

&

LAUREN WAS OUTSIDE DUMPING DISHWATER ONE July day toward the time the men would be coming home from practice when the small cottage caught her eye. It was so adorable: miniature and perfect. She walked slowly around it, admiring the way someone had lovingly cultivated flowers up the walls, decades ago.

She'd made a full circle around the cottage and was looking up the mountain toward where she, Jessica, and Katherine had fled a year before when she saw someone hiking down. Out of place in his multicolored clothes, he was quite distant yet. She couldn't tell for certain, but she thought maybe he was a time traveler like her and the other women in the house, all save for Senga.

Careful to mind where he was and which direction he was walking, she opened the front door.

"Jessica, Katherine, Amy! Come look."

The other women came running and looked where Lauren was pointing. There were gasps.

"I think he's wearing tie-dye."

"He is!"

"Why are there so many time travelers?"

"Yeah," said Lauren. "I've never before heard of the druids bringing so many people back in time all at once. Kelsey should finally be done with that assignment and be able to contact us any day now. We'll ask her."

They still kept their eyes on the hippie, but Katherine put a gentle hand on Lauren's wrist.

"Will she be able to tell us anything? I mean, she is one of them, right?"

"She is and she isn't," Lauren mused. "I mean yeah, she has the training and the power, and she gets it from the druids. But I told you, she didn't know what was going on. She thought she was just getting a doctorate in Celtic artwork. So we can trust Kelsey. I do."

This time it was Amy who laid the gentle hand on Lauren.

"But Kelsey's an old friend of yours, right? Someone you've known since you were thirteen?"

Lauren didn't like the way this line of questioning was going, so she just stood there silently and nodded a bit, pointedly watching tie-dye guy come down the mountain.

"He'll be here in a few minutes, and I know he sees us looking at him. Let's plan what we're going to say."

Jessica came over and put a supportive arm around Lauren's shoulders, giving Amy a smile that said 'Enough.'

"Good idea. I'll invite him in so it'll be harder for him to leave, and then we'll just be super curious and ask him questions. Sound good?"

Katherine nodded

"Sounds good to me."

Amy nodded and smiled at Katherine.

"To me too."

They waited quietly, and when he reached them, he spoke to them in Gaelic, plainly mistaking them for people of this time. Lauren supposed that wasn't too surprising. They were wearing clothes made in this time: summer linen leines with huge coordinating woolen shawls.

"Wull met," he said with a slight nod to Jessica, the best-dressed among them. "My people call me Sky Blue, but ye lasses may call me Sky."

They all exchanged a look, eager to take advantage of his assumption that they were of this time to see what he might let slip, thinking they would be none the wiser.

"Wull met. I am Jessica, the lady o' Cresh Manor, and these are my friends: Lauren, Katherine, and Amy. Will ye come in? We wull be supping soon, and 'tis a long walk ower the mountain."

Sky looked uncertain, but when they all started walking toward the house, he followed them inside and took the seat Jessica gestured to, at the table.

Lauren casually moved over to stand watch at the back door so Sky couldn't escape that way. She knew the men would be coming up the pathway through the trees toward the front door. They would intercept him if he left that way.

Katherine met Jessica's eyes.

Jessica nodded at her subtly.

It was an understatement to say that Katherine, a top salesperson in the 21st Century, had a way with words.

"'Tis a rarity for us tae get a visitor from yon castle. Dae ye come with news?"

But before Sky could answer, little Amena came out of the kitchen. Wide-eyed at the sight of Sky, she ran over to him and fiddled with his tie-dyed outfit.

"Braw clothes! Are ye a time traveler too?"

Chapter Four

Taran patted his brother's back as they headed away from fight practice.

"We hae did wull fortifying Inverurie. 'Tis tae the good."

"Aye," Leif said, nodding, but a sigh gave the lie to his nod. He was just trying to be encouraging. Meanwhile, as usual he was glancing anxiously at the road from the West, looking for signs of the messenger who would call them all out to join the earl in battle.

Luag took a turn, fixing Leif with his charming smile and holding out his hand to the town behind them.

"Yer duty lies here. These people are yer responsibility."

Leif mustered a tiny wry grin for his friend.

"What? Nay jesting this time? Hae ye lost yer touch?"

Luag chuckled in acknowledgment that Leif had made a rare jest of his own, but then his face was serious.

"It burdens me tae see ye sae, doubting yerself. Ye are a fine leader. Inverurie is blessed tae hae ye. I mean that, or I would na be staying tae fight under yer leadership, now would I?"

They were halfway through the barley fields now, and Taran imagined he could smell their supper cooking, all the way up the hill.

Leif clapped a firm hand over Taran's shoulders and changed the subject.

"And what news from ye? Hae ye not e'en yet proposed marriage tae Lauren?"

Taran made a face at Leif that said 'Far be it from ye tae be uncomfortable, sae let's just throw the talk onto my discomfort, eh?'

Leif nodded sideways in a 'ye are welcome' way, grinning. He and Luag were both looking at Taran expectantly, making him feel the need to say something.

Lauren still hadn't told everyone her secret, and Taran had made a promise not to be the one to do so. But he had also promised himself he would go no further in courting her until she had. They were in a stalemate. But he couldn't tell them that, so he said the first thing that came to mind.

"Lauren isna ripe yet for the picking. I will need tae cultivate her some more."

The other men laughed at his simile.

Luag fixed him with a cutting grin.

"Nae more insisting ye are na interested in her? leaving me all alone, are ye?"

Taran shoved the Isles man playfully.

"Ye are nay more alone than I, whether ye ken it or na."

They walked for a time without talking, and then Taran heard something. He stopped to hear it better. The others did as well.

There.

Peals of female laughter rang out from Cresh Manor, along with the distinct sound of an unfamiliar male voice.

The lasses must have left the windows and the doors open, but the male voice was what had Taran on edge. He exchanged inquisitive glances with Luag and Leif, but neither of them knew what was going on either.

They all broke into a run up the steep pathway through the woods.

When they entered the manor, Taran knew it had indeed been Senga's stew he smelled from afar. A tiny part of him rejoiced. Senga's stew was legendary throughout Inverurie. The rest of Taran, however, was on high alert, scanning the room for any signs of distress.

But on the contrary, the lasses were all at the table with the stranger, who sat taking his ease with a tankard of ale, his leg over the arm of the chair and repeatedly stealing looks at the beautiful Katherine.

The stranger's multicolored clothing was so odd that if Taran hadn't met a dozen time travelers in the past four months, he would have been quite mystified, perhaps even shocked. As it was, he found himself staring. How many people were there going to be from other times, wandering around, and why?

This new one was bragging about his adventures.

"Aye, I hae been in this time half a year. They treat me wull, and I am starting tae think I willna go back. Excepting that they are all sae darn bloodthirsty."

Jessica went to Leif, her husband, and he pulled out her chair for her, then sat down at the head of the table.

Lauren met Taran's eyes, beckoning him to sit across from her, which he did. This meant they could communicate with the gestures they had taught each other over the past year while playing a game in the evenings after supper, that game she loved and called Charades.

"Supper is ready to be served," Senga announced.

"Good," said Leif, who then bowed his head and said the blessing.

While Jessica made introductions, Senga served the stew. And then Leif leaned toward the stranger.

"Ye say they treat ye well, Sky Blue?"

"Aye," said Sky, with an air of self-importance.

"And pray tell, who are 'they'?"

Sky turned his head sideways and smiled.

"Ye wull ken I canna tell ye."

Amena spoke up with her shrill excited voice.

"Jessica is gaun'ae stay here in oor time also, ye ken, because she's married tae Leif. She's part o' oor family now!"

Sky ignored the child, speaking right over her.

"They hae big plans for me. Objects they say I can find for them. Some aught tae dae with my aura, thinks I. Hardly anyone can see auras, ye ken, but they hae people who can. Wull, they can travel through time, sae that's na sae verra surprising—"

Leif interrupted sky right back.

"Now I think ye speak o' a different people than ye foremaist brought tae mind. When ye said they were bloodthirsty, I did think ye meant the Laird o' the Isles and his men. But only the druids can travel through time."

With that same sense of self-importance, Sky spoke through the bite of stew he just put in his mouth.

"I telt ye, I canna say who they are. They close my mouth whene'er I try—"

Taran met Lauren's eyes.

She widened hers, recognizing her own plight.

Taran nodded.

Sky blathered on, oblivious.

"But most o' them are warriors. They hae conquered a great deal o' this land, moving constantly farther east. Their jewelry isna anything like yers." He indicated Taran and Leif. "'Tis more like his." He nodded at Luag.

When Sky pointed at Luag, the stranger's rudeness was the least of Taran's concerns. The Laird o' the of the Isles and the druids were allied! This was...

Taran met his brother's eyes and received a curt nod of agreement. The two of them looked over at Luag, and his face showed fear as well.

The lasses didn't seem to grasp what this meant. Perhaps they didn't realize were Luag was from.

Lauren asked Taran with their gestures, "What's wrong?"

Taran signed back to her, "Our two enemies have allied."

She gave him a sickened face.

He nodded solemnly.

Oblivious to all this interaction, Sky pompously ate his stew and slurped his wine, all the while ogling Katherine the beautiful. It was so bad, Luag even looked over at Katherine to see how she was taking this, with an eye, Taran knew, of putting a stop to it if she was at all affronted.

Good man, Luag.

But Katherine signed to him, "Certies ye jest. At home, I get far worse treatment from men every hour of every day. I wull let you know if I need help."

Meanwhile, Sky was nattering on. Taran was ignoring him until Sky's words launched a volley that caught Taran right in the throat:

"'Tis glad I am I got here ahead of them. I only just barely did. They're holed up in the castle just east o' here, ye ken..."

Laird Donald had overtaken Laird Ualraig's castle! Taran felt a surge of battle heat race through his veins.

Leif jumped up from the table and wasted no time in going outside to play a rare tune on his small pipes. It called the militia to muster after their families had gone to bed. The battle plan where they all left after their families were asleep would be enacted tonight.

On hearing the unfamiliar tune, Lauren raised her eyebrows at Taran.

He signed a lie, his first ever to her.

"There will be a meeting first thing on the morrow to discuss this news and plan our course."

And then Taran got up from the table and gave Senga a signal they'd only discussed and never used.

Their old cook took his little sister by the hand. "Say goodnight tae everyone, Amena dear. Ye wull come sleep in my room sae Sky can hae yers."

The two disappeared into the kitchen, and a few minutes later, Senga came out with a wine decanter and replenished everyone's glasses. Taran, Leif, and Luag went into the kitchen one by one and switched theirs before drinking.

The hour that followed was long, listening to Sky.

"I took a semester o' medieval waurld history afore I dropped out o' college." He yawned noisily, stretching his arms out over his head. "This is good wine. May I hae more? They say my knowledge is useful tae them: dates and such, alliances, the outcomes o' battles. I am verra useful tae them. They wull keep me a long time. The others are just..." He yawned again. "Wull, they willna let me say..."

The lasses fought their sleepiness, but at long last they all excused themselves to go up to bed.

Sky —who had drunk four glasses of the special wine in an hour— fell asleep on his face at the table.

Taran, Leif, and Luag gave the lasses half an hour to fall deeply asleep, and then Leif nodded to Senga on their way out. They carried Sky with them to keep him from rushing on ahead to warn the Laird of the Isles of their coming, when he awoke.

The meadow where the militia met was distant enough that no one could hear them or see them, up over the rise of the northern hill. Each time someone new arrived, he would ask those already there the same question:

"Where lies the threat?"

And each time, the last one to arrive would tell the new arrival.

"The threat surrounds us. Laird Donald o' the Isles has teamed up with the druids! They hae taken Laird Ualraig's castle, along with every other settlement in their path. The only hope for Inverurie is if we bring the fight tae them."

Chapter Five

Galdus fumed. Why had Lauren drunk that wine despite his urging her not to? He had to get better control of her! Now he would have to wait until he was able to wake her from her sullied wine stupor, and that would take hours! Time was slipping away, and if she didn't catch up with the warriors and accompany them to the Battle of Harlaw, this whole trip would be for nothing.

❦

LAUREN RAN TO KELSEY AS SOON AS SHE SAW HER old friend, who was visiting in her dream. Jessica and Katherine were here as well. Kelsey had shaken their hands, and so she was able to orchestrate dreams for them as well. Not so with Amy, but they would fill their new friend in.

"I'm so glad to see you!" Lauren said. "What took you so long? Never mind. You're here now, and that's what matters. What can you tell us about the coming conflict? When will it be? Who's involved? Are Taran, Leif, or Luag mentioned by name?"

Kelsey returned Lauren's hug warmly and then turned to face the three of them, noting with a smile they were all sitting on their thrones this time. She had discovered that this ancient Celtic palace under Dunskey Castle was the only place their dreams couldn't be spied upon by other dream walkers. It was very convenient, as that was where Kelsey worked in the waking world. She had a strong connection with the place.

"The Battle of Harlaw happens in a few days," Kelsey told them. "The Laird of the Isles is met by Glen Allen's Earl of Mar in a field near the very town you're in. The losses are so heavy that both sides retreat. It's considered a draw by most historians. None of your men are mentioned by name, and you're right, that's a good thing."

Katherine tossed her hair and smiled sweetly at Kelsey.

"Jessica here is married to Leif, so yeah, he's her man. And everything points to Lauren getting engaged to Taran soon, from what you've told us about men's behavior in this time. But Luag and I? We are so not together. I'm not staying in this backward time. It's been a fun trip and all, but I'm overdue to go home, and I will, as soon as I feel I can leave these two. Please tell me you did secure me a leave of absence from PenUlt? And you made sure my bills were paid so my credit will still be excellent when I get home?"

Not at all taken in by Katherine's charm, Kelsey nodded in a matter-of-fact way.

"I did. Your credit and your job are safe. You can return whenever you get back." She grinned mischievously. "You're dating a famous musician, and he's taken you on tour. I've been sending postcards from you to your family."

Lauren enjoyed watching Katherine squirm at this news. Ms. In-Control was mighty uncomfortable, and it was medicine for the soul, to watch it. But Lauren had to give Katherine credit. She sucked it up.

"Thank you," Katherine said with a forced nod of acknowledgment. "I can work with that." But then she got an inquisitive look on her face and raised her head again toward Kelsey. "What if my father contacts the musician's agent? Won't that blow my cover?"

Lauren had known Kelsey twelve years now, so she saw what Katherine didn't: Kelsey was getting annoyed. She had handled it. She was done with this part of the conversation and had other news to share.

All Kelsey said to Katherine was, "We made arrangements with a Celtic Rock band. Don't worry about it."

Lauren turned her head so that Katherine wouldn't see her smirk at Jessica, who smiled in return. But Lauren wasn't so smug when Kelsey then turned her determined stare on her.

"Lauren, you need to tell them what's going on with you and Galdus. If you don't tell them, then I will."

Normally, Lauren insisted on privacy. She didn't stay friends with anyone who couldn't keep a secret. But Kelsey was right. This affected her other friends.

"You know what?" Lauren said. "That would be easier for me. Go ahead and tell them. Please. I really wanted to time travel, but it's not worth it. Sometimes I wish we'd never come, but then I think of Taran…"

Lauren looked Jessica in the eye and then Katherine, trying to convey to them how sorry she was for putting them in danger.

"On second thought," she told Kelsey, "I'll tell them."

She looked her friends in the eye once more, pleading with her eyes for them to hear her out.

"Taran wasn't trying to propose marriage to me in the cottage. He caught me raging at Galdus, demanded an explanation, and conceded to hear it in private. So here it is."

Lauren swallowed, but she kept choking up anyway, the precursor to tears.

"Galdus is getting more and more control over me. I seem to be safe from his influence here in Kelsey's dream, but in the real world he often keeps me from saying certain things, and... And just last night he tried to prevent me from drinking my wine. I could feel him trying to control my arm. I was only just barely able to get control of it for myself and drink my wine anyway. That's a minor thing, but can you imagine what might happen if he got total physical control? It scares me to death. But we need him in order to get home, unless..."

Lauren looked at Kelsey and relaxed a bit.

"Unless you can get us home?"

Kelsey nodded.

"I can't do it myself, but I know several people who can. Don't worry about that. If you want to go home, then I'll make sure you get there."

Katherine looked worried.

"But what if something happens to you, Kelsey? If we can't talk to you here in the dream and we no longer have Lauren's magic time traveling dagger, then what?"

Lauren expected Kelsey to answer impatiently, but she looked thoughtful.

"You're right. I'd better tell them to check on you in the event anything does happen to me. Satisfied?"

Katherine fixed angry eyes on Lauren, only briefly turning to tell Kelsey yes. "I can't believe you dragged us both into this, Lauren. We're all in danger, not just you. What do you think is going to happen if he finally does take you over? You think he's gonna make us all sell Girl Scout cookies? No! He's going to find a way to get us into slavery as well. That's what greed does.

Greedy people are never satisfied. They always want more, more, more—"

Jessica spoke right over Katherine.

"Katherine, we need to live in the cure, not in the disease. Lauren knows she messed up. She admits it. Rubbing her nose in it isn't going to fix anything. We need to free her from this druid dagger before he takes her over any more than he has."

At first, Katherine kept berating Lauren.

"You didn't stop to think why a druid would tell someone to give you a magic dagger, did you? No, you didn't..."

But gradually, Jessica's words must have sunk in, because Katherine stopped talking, nodded, and then finally gave Lauren a little hug. There were tears in her eyes.

"Jessica's right. We're here for you."

Lauren was crying too now, but they were tears of relief. Her friends were with her. And now they knew why she couldn't talk sometimes. Why hadn't she told them during Kelsey's last dream, or the one before that? This was going to make life so much easier.

Jessica turned to Kelsey.

"You must know how to get her free of this ancient druid's control. What do we do?"

Lauren felt herself waking up, and that didn't usually happen in the middle of one of Kelsey's dreams. She struggled to stay with her old friend from the Renaissance Faire, hoping she would have an answer.

But Kelsey was shaking her head no.

"I don't know. Imbuing objects with power or presence isn't my gift. I have a lead on someone who knows, but she's on an assignment. My bosses won't let me contact her yet. But I will get help for you, Lauren. Resist—"

That was the end of the dream, because Lauren woke up to Galdus cackling in her mind.

"Now you decide to interact?" she chided.

His answer was far more forceful than she expected.

"Get up and get moving! Ye hae tae find the men! 'Tis only just barely sunrise, and they're nowhere tae be heard in the house. They've gone off somewhere, and ye need tae catch up tae them! They had that auld lass Senga put some aught in yer wine tae make ye sleep! Hurry!"

She rubbed the sleep from her bleary eyes.

"Galdus, I ken ye hae been lying tae me all along, but this lie takes the cake. Ye expect me tae believe that these men who are protecting me would drug me? Losing yer touch, ye are. That is the last thing they would dae."

"Where are they then, seeing how ye ken them sae wull? Ye dinna hear them. I can tell. They drugged ye sae they could leave with nary ye. Arise and catch up w' them!"

Lauren rolled over on her other side and prepared to go back to sleep.

"As if I do what you say."

In her attempt to get comfy, she plumped up the pillow. Turned it over. Rolled over onto her back and pulled the covers up to her chin. She lay there for a few minutes.

"Thanks a lot, Galdus. You have gone and woken me up too early. I'm missing out on an hour of sleep."

I might as well go down and help Senga with breakfast, after I use the water closet.

She thought this last part to herself and not to Galdus, determining not to speak to him until the next time she needed his help.

Yeah, he's better just used and not heard.

That thought made her chuckle as, expecting to see the men gathered around the table talking as usual while Senga made breakfast, she barged through the door to the stairs. And froze. No one was there.

That's right, Leif called a militia meeting for this morning. That's where they are. Awful early.

"Senga? Could ye use my help in the kitchen this morning? I'm up early."

Amena came out of the kitchen rubbing her eyes, poor thing. She cried sometimes when she missed her parents.

Because Galdus could read the thoughts of anyone Lauren had touched, she didn't dare hug the girl. She made do with a sympathetic look.

"Aw, did everyone go tae toon and leave ye all alone?"

The little girl sat down on the kitchen hearth to warm herself.

"Nay, Senga went doon tae the well, but Leif and them didna go tae toon. They hae gone off tae battle."

Chapter Six

The trek over two mountains to Laird Ualraig's castle was difficult under the best of conditions, but Taran had never taken it by night before. The moon loaned its faint glow through the clouds so it wasn't completely dark, the horses carried their burdens, and all the men of Inverurie were familiar with the trail, but it was still slow going. The only relief was when Leif stopped from time to time to play his small pipes. So far, they hadn't heard any response.

To make matters worse, Sky had woken up. The man bragged incessantly. And affrontingly.

"Laird Donald o' the Isles has ten thousand men, ye ken. He is a real laird, unlike Leif here, who is merely flattered sae he wull bide in this backwater farmland. Though I will say they dae give him beautiful lasses..."

Behind Sky's back, Taran met Leif's eyes, curled his lip in fierceness, and mimed hitting Sky over the head, to relieve them all of the insult of listening to him.

Leif smiled, but shook his head, gesturing that they couldn't risk killing the traitor, as his knowledge was of use to them. Besides, they needed all the horses to carry supplies.

Taran looked, and sure enough, their one horse had been carrying Sky, but now that he could walk it was loaded up with supplies the men had been carrying. He nodded to Leif, signing, "Aye, the men need tae save their strength for battle."

So Taran put up with the braggart, but the man's ramblings were unbearable. Leif constantly had to sign to the others not to knock the man out —or strangle him. They needed him to stay with them and remain compliant. Useless to their enemy, but an unexpected source of news for them.

Sky's opinion of himself was anything but news.

"I'm Laird Donald's personal guest for meals, ye ken. Aye, I'm a valuable member o' his army. Sae valuable that he let me scout on ahead for any lasses, afore the rest o' them got intae yer toon. And I found three lovely specimens. Too bad they were sae wull guarded. I was really looking forward tae having my fun with them, ye ken?"

Leif had stopped to play his small pipes.

Taran had stopped being hopeful.

But then the response came, distant, on top of the next mountain.

Taran smiled at Leif, signing, "The Wolf is smart. Taking the high ground above the castle will help prevent them from being attacked by surprise in their sleep."

With his small pipes still in hand and a pleased look on his face, Leif gave the signal for secretiveness while looking askance at Sky, then signed, "Tell those behind you."

Taran proceeded to do so using their warrior hand signals, which had been much augmented since Lauren arrived and taught them her game of Charades.

But everyone signed back that obviously they knew not to tell the traitor their allies were on top of the next mountain with nearly fifteen hundred knights. What did he take them for?

Seeming oblivious to all this, Sky just kept blathering on about how important he was to their enemy. But when they got near the bottom of the mountain, he edged his way toward the rear guard.

Taran followed, signing to his brother, "Sky expects an attack. Look at him retreating. I'll keep an eye on him."

Leif nodded, signaling for Taran to hurry Sky away so he wouldn't notice Leif warning the Wolf.

Once Taran had followed Sky to the back of their militia, he faintly heard Leif's small pipes and the response. Good. A contingent of men had come down the other side of the far mountain, some with bows, most with swords.

Sky made a show of taking a piss.

Taran joined him, ostensibly to keep him company, but really to keep an eye on him. Unlike Sky, Taran didn't like hiding behind everyone, out of the action.

He could hear the conflict up ahead: yelping in surprise as the Isles men who had thought to ambush the militia were hit by arrows, the militia yelling as they charged, the clash of swords, and the grunts as men fell. It was over before Taran and Sky even reached the site.

All the ambushers were dead.

Alvin was injured, and Leif sent him home.

They learned that the Wolf had passed away six years ago. His son by the same name, Alasdair Stewart, Earl of Mar, now led his men. Some of them were greeting the townsmen, and Taran stood by Sky and watched. Leif went over and shook forearms with their leader, a Lovel clansman named Calum, whom Taran had only seen once before, at a gathering of the clans when he was barely old enough to be a warrior. The two talked amiably for a moment and then both turned and signaled for everyone to climb up the second mountain to the earl's encampment.

Taran didn't fancy staying up half the night after not sleeping the night before, but Leif and Calum were right. With the Isles men so near on the other side of the battlefield at the bottom of this canyon, it was far too dangerous to camp down here where they usually did on the way to Ualraig's.

When Luag joined Taran and Sky for this climb, Sky woke up a bit from his obliviousness to stare.

"Aye, the more I look at ye, the more different ye seem from the men here in the middle o' Scotland. Ye look more like the men from the isles."

Taran wasn't worried about their friend. Luag had been gifted with a silver tongue, and he did not disappoint.

"That's because I hail from there. At least I belong here in this time."

Sky bristled with indignation.

"I belong. Laird Donald has about adopted me as his son, he dotes on me sae. Why just the other day..." And off he went on his bragging.

Behind Sky's back, Luag signed to Taran, "'Tis a good thing none o' the earl's men are back here, or 'tis a certainty they would kill the fool."

Taran signed back, "Why have na we done sae?"

Luag grinned and signed, "Because the fool is sae useful as a source o' knowledge about the enemy, the way he blathers on."

"At least we can tie him up and gag him once we get tae camp," Taran signed.

Luag didn't sign back to that one. He just nodded grimly. And they did just that before joining one of the campfires to have some supper, after all the knights had fed their horses. The night was long and cold even with the ability to bundle up. Taran snickered to think how cold Sky must be feeling.

In the morning, conscience got the best of Taran, and he got an extra helping of parritch to bring over to the prisoner.

But Sky was gone.

Taran ran through the camp looking for Leif. He found him at Calum's campfire.

"Leif! Sky is gone."

Leif stood and threw his arms wide.

"I thought ye had the sense tae tie him up!"

"We did. The bonds are still tied. 'Tis as if the man dissolved out o' them like suet melting through a net."

Calum raised his brows at Leif.

"The Isles traitor ye informed me o', the one who lured ye intae the ambush?"

"Aye."

Calum put his hand on Leif's shoulder. "Recall that they hae the druids with them. All manner o' things will be possible which usually are na." He turned. "Well met, Taran. Ye were but a lad the last time I did see ye. Dinna Fash. 'Tis not the usual sort o' treachery we deal with here. Have a care from now on, eh?"

Taran stepped forward and shook forearms with Calum. "Aye. And I thank ye for yer forgiveness." He looked over at Leif, half afraid his brother wasn't going to forgive him. But he should've known better.

Leif stood as well and came over to clap his hand

on Taran's shoulder. "Calum has the right o' it. 'Tis sorry I am for my lack o' faith in ye." He turned to Luag. "And in ye as well, old friend."

Now that attention had been put on Luag, Taran noticed that practically all the earl's men had gathered around to stare at their Isles friend with wary eyes. Taran didn't blame them, but...

He needn't have worried. Angus came forward and put his arm around Luag. And then Aiden did. And more, until Luag was surrounded by the men from Inverurie.

The earl himself approached, and everyone's head nodded toward him. Fists went to hearts in the warrior's salute.

Obviously curious about the clump of men but acting unperturbed, the earl walked up to Leif.

"'Twas happy we were tae hear yer pipes, Leif. Glad we are ye hae joined us."

Leif put his fist to his heart in salute.

"Glad I am tae see ye again, Alasdair, but sorry for yer father's loss."

The earl blinked in acknowledgement.

Leif continued, "I would introduce ye tae a dear friend o' mine who has been helping us guard Inverurie against the verra druids who hae now joined with Donald o' the Isles."

Alasdair Stewart, Glen Allen's Earl of Mar, inclined his head. "Please dae." He raised his voice so that all around could hear. "Please dae introduce yer friend who has helped defend Inverurie against the druids, Leif. For any friend o' Inverurie is a friend tae me."

There was murmuring among the earl's men.

"He does na ken 'tis an Isles man."

"Nay, and there will be Hell tae pay when he does."

"Aye, just ye watch."

But it quickly died when the Earl stared his men down.

Leif turned to the clump of men and gestured for them to open up and let Luag out. he waited a moment.

Luag came out. Looking calm and strangely regal, he too raised his fist to his heart in homage to the Wolf's son.

Leif went over and put his arm around Luag, turning the two of them to face everyone gathered around.

"This is my dear friend Luag. He is a member o' my militia, and any affront tae him is an affront tae me."

"Who is Leif?" whispered one of the younger men to one of the older men nearby.

"He's the Laird over Inverurie," the older man stage-whispered back, keeping his eyes on Leif. "We may need tae retreat tae his lands, so we would do well tae stay in his good graces, ye ken?"

The younger man nodded, looking at Leif. "'Tis a

complicated thing, gaun'ae battle. I thought 'twould be just fighting, but my mind is coming intae it."

All of the older men laughed, and one of them mussed the young man's hair.

The young man scowled, which made them all laugh again. A few of them lunged at him, and he flinched away.

A frantic scout ran up, no older that he of the tousled hair.

"A messenger from the Laird o' the Isles!"

Alistair laughed. "I suppose I had better go talk tae him." He looked at Leif, Taran, and Luag, holding his hand out in front of him. "Come, fill my mind with the druids' methods o' attack."

As they walked, Leif filled Alasdair in on the manner in which the druids had burned their winter grain stores. He also told how the druids knew that Leif's wife and her friends were ... special ... and how the druids had tried several times to capture the lasses.

They went to the outskirts of the camp, where two men held the messenger by the arms, also a young warrior. Taran thought he was doing a good job hiding his discomfort and the fear he must have felt at being captive.

The earl stepped out in front. "I am Alasdair Stewart, Earl o' Mar. And ye are?"

The young man stood a little straighter. "I am Ian MacDonald."

The earl raised his eyebrows. "Donald sent his son?"

"Nay, his cousin."

"I hear ye hae a message for me."

"Aye." The young man swallowed, looking around at all who surrounded him and no doubt gauging his chances of escape. And finding them slim. "Laird Donald bids me tell you that if you will surrender your lands to him, then he will spare your lives... And... And the lives of your wives and children." The young man was shaking in fear now, but he still stood straight and proud.

The earl pretended to think about this for a moment. Letting the young man quake in fear.

"That is na acceptable tae me, but I will give Donald one more chance tae come tae terms. I dinna wish for bloodshed. I will meet with him at sunset out in yon field. We each bring three men with us, nae more. If anyone is within bow range, mind, the meeting is off."

He turned to the men blocking the messenger's path and gestured for them to part ways.

They parted immediately.

The young messenger turned around and ran.

The men laughed.

Alistair turned and watched the young messenger run until he descended over the side of the mountain, out of sight. He turned to Taran, Leif, and Luag. "Carry the white flag for me this evening."

Their fists flew to their hearts.

They stood watch most of the day, but they had plenty of opportunities to greet those they'd only seen at the last gathering: Irvings, Lesleys, Lovels, Maules, Morays, and Stirlings. Sunset came all too soon.

Taran started out carrying the white flag.

But Luag reached out his hand. "I canna think o' anything more fitting than if the islander shows up with ye highlanders carrying the verra symbol o' cooperation. Can ye?"

Taran handed it to him. "Nay, I canna."

Leif noticed their exchange, but seeing that the earl was intent only on scoping out the open field ahead of them, he just shrugged.

After all, they had been brought along to keep an eye out for any threats so that they could shield the Earl, and this they did. It was the longest mile Taran had ever walked on level ground. Even when they arrived at the meeting site and could hear the earl and the laird exchanging pleasantries, Taran was still on high alert, searching his third of the area for any sign of a threat. He watched Donald's three men just as closely, and they watched him, Leif, and Luag.

It became more and more clear that Donald wouldn't settle for anything less than conquering all of Scotland.

"Yer people may hae lived on these lands thousands o' years," Donald told Alasdair, "but yer ancestors were conquerors back afore the Romans named ye Picts. Ye are nae better than us."

Alasdair tried to be diplomatic. "Yet we are speaking neither yer language nor ours either, but that o' the Gaels. And yer Viking king o' Norway ceded the isles tae Scotland in 1266. He was paid handsomely..."

Taran almost fainted, he was so afraid.

Not for himself.

No, he was afraid for Lauren, because for a brief moment she was visible to him. She and Katherine and Jessica were standing just a few feet away there on the grass. The ancient druid in her dagger had brought them there unseen, so why had they appeared, even just for a moment?

More importantly, had anyone else seen them?

Taran scrutinized everyone, including Laird Donald, looking for any sign that they'd seen the lasses. What would they do if they did? He was so afraid for Lauren that he was in danger of swooning like a woman, but he relaxed a bit when he saw that Laird Donald hadn't seen the lasses. Whew, his men weren't reacting, either.

Luag and Leif looked at Taran with questions in their eyes, but Taran didn't dare take his attention off their enemies. What if the evil druid revealed the lasses again? He had to be ready to defend them.

However, while Donald hadn't noticed the lasses, it soon became quite apparent he noticed Taran staring at him.

Donald stepped out into the area between his three men and Alasdair's, glaring at Taran.

"I see the challenge in yer stare." He drew his sword from the harness on his back and stood ready. "If ye are sae brave, come and fight me one-on-one. We shall let that determine the outcome o' oor differences."

Donald was now facing the place where Lauren had appeared with her friends.

Taran ran in between Donald and the lasses. He did it without waiting to see what Alasdair thought. This was his fault. He shouldn't have stared at the laird so openly. He would protect them.

Behind Taran, Alasdair's voice rang out for all to hear.

"Surely ye want the lands for goods that ye are na able tae grow on the isles. Let us work up trade routes, instead o' shedding each other's blood...."

But Donald didn't even look at Alasdair. He attacked.

Before Taran could finish drawing his sword, he felt a pain across his belly, doubled over, and went down.

Chapter Seven

Lauren tried to scream when Taran was cut down, but Jessica put a hand over her mouth. Lauren tried to run to Taran, but Katherine held her by the elbows. The three of them had lain down after Taran saw them, hiding in the tall grass just in case. Through Galdus, they communicated inside their minds, where they didn't need to speak Gaelic.

"Let me go!" Lauren cried.

Jessica's hold on Lauren's mouth was gentle but firm. "Not yet. Wait till the others go away."

Lauren struggled, crying out in her mind, "He's still breathing! We can save him if we hurry! You're a nurse, Jessica. Didn't you take an oath that says you have to help when someone needs it? Taran needs help, and you can save him! Even I know that every minute counts when someone's bleeding out. We have to go now! We have to!"

Katherine kept a firm hold on Lauren, preventing her from getting up. "Lauren, think! Galdus revealed us to the men once. He can do it again. Nothing says he has to keep on hiding us at all. We will go to Taran, but Jess is right. Wait till the other men are gone. I know you love Taran, but you need to stay safe. Think!"

Lauren was sobbing fat, heavy tears now, through her nose because Jessica was still covering her mouth. The two friends hugged her close and held her while she cried for what seemed like hours.

At long last, the other men had left the field and only Leif was with Taran.

"I will go and get a litter tae carry him home," Luag said as he left. He didn't look hopeful, but he didn't know the extent of modern medicine.

So sure was she that they could save Taran if they only got there in time that Lauren dropped her friends' hands to run to him faster.

She could still hear their thoughts. Galdus only needed contact in order to make them invisible. He could telepathically reach anyone she had ever touched, up to a radius of ten feet from her. Even inside a man-made structure, he wasn't limited in the ways that corporal druids were. The dagger acted like a battery, storing up magical energy that he could use whenever. No, Galdus's limitation was that he needed a human to carry him around. He lacked mobility on his own.

As soon as Lauren saw how bad Taran was hurt,

she screamed out to Jessica in her mind, "Do something!"

But Jessica was crying too, shaking her head and raising up her hands in a helpless gesture to both Leif and Lauren. "'Oh Lauren, 'tis far worse than I thought. I canna save him. He can still hear ye though. 'Tis best ye say yer goodbyes."

Lauren and Leif both threw themselves down on the ground near Taran's head, the only place it looked like they wouldn't hurt him by touching him. Leif took his brother's hand, while as gently as she could, Lauren cradled Taran's face in her lap.

And then tears cascaded down her face, because although Taran was too injured to speak, she could now hear his thoughts in her mind.

"Leif, carry on for me, my brother. Lauren! Och, Lauren. I wanted tae marry ye and for us tae live in the wee cottage together, happy the rest o' oor days. It is na tae be. Ye must go home tae yer own time and yer own people sae ye will be safe from all this bloodshed. I love ye, and I will see ye in Heaven one day. Till then, live yer life happily. Dinna mourn for me. Dinna try tae remain faithful tae my memory. 'Tis a waste o' the time ye hae tae live. Be happy for me, for I'm going home. God be with ye, Lauren. Remember, be happy."

But Lauren didn't want to let go of him. She wanted the life he had designed for them together. Not knowing if she was screaming out loud or her in her mind —and not caring— she screamed nonetheless, bending down to kiss Taran's mouth with such anguish that Leif let go and stood up again to hold his own wife and give Lauren and his brother what privacy he could.

"Galdus, do something!" Lauren screamed inside her mind at the druid in her dagger.

He gave her his evil chuckle. "Och, now ye need me."

Now in Leif's arms, comforting him rather than being comforted, Jessica dug around in her purse. "I have some aught I can give him for the pain, but 'tis all I can do."

But Katherine grabbed Lauren by the arms and tried to pull her away from Taran. "They hae seen us! They return! We hae tae go!"

At the same time as Katherine said this, the world started swirling, blurring, and whirling past Lauren, Katherine, and Taran as if they were in a whirlpool underwater, and Lauren smiled, hoping they were traveling back in time to when Taran wasn't injured. She knew it for certain when she saw Taran's wound mending, and once it was no longer bleeding, she clutched at him in a joy that overwhelmed all the despair she had felt moments before.

❧

LUAG SCREAMED IN SHOCK. ALL OF A SUDDEN Katherine was right there in front of him, hunched over between him and Donald. He lunged, grabbing hold of her waist and trying to pull her away to safety as she clung to something there on the ground. What was it?

But then Luag forgot about whatever lay on the ground.

He could hear Katherine's thoughts!

"I've had enough and want to go home!" she pleaded in her mind, thinking of the strangest place ever. It had the largest beaches, but it was a city of metal and glass. A pier jutted out into the ocean, and on it were brightly lit monstrosities that moved! The sign at the top of it read Santa Monica. Was it in Spain, then? She thought of her home, and it was like a spot on a shelf above a cafe between two shops, which were themselves squished into a row of shops which were all in one enormous long building that faced another such building across a huge stone walkway. She couldn't see the ocean from her home, but she could smell it, so it was nearby.

The world did flips around Luag, as if he were swimming on the seashore, being churned by the waves. Someone grabbed onto his back, and he lurched to get the man off him even as he held onto Katherine and pulled her away toward safety.

Abruptly, he no longer heard her mind inside his. No longer saw what she imagined. He didn't need to. He and Katherine were there, in the place she had imagined.

The ocean air was pleasantly balmy, but everything else made him uncomfortable.

He didn't understand anything he saw except the hundreds of people who walked past him, so for a few moments he focused on them. They were all in such a rush! And they were rude.

"Watch where you're going!"

"Get out of the way!"

"Wrong way, buddy."

"Go back to the Renaissance Faire!"

Luag would have said something back, only his jaw hung open. They were all wearing so little clothing! Nothing was left to his imagination. The women wore even less than the men, less than undergarments. Only the barest parts of their bodies were covered up, and he could see more skin than anything else. None of them seemed to be at all bothered by it. Well, a few of the men were looking at the women, but appreciatively, not in any sort of panic that the women had lost their clothing.

These people set him on edge, and so he looked away from them, at everything else.

The surface they were standing on — for it could not be called the ground — was hard like stone, but it was flat and smooth like an earthenware plate. Everyone was walking around on it without comment, so it must've been normal for them, but it was not normal for Luag. The surface was white or very light gray and now that he looked closer it was marked with a series of lines that crisscrossed each other. The more he looked at it, the more aggravated he grew. It made him feel overcome with the urge to bend over and scrape it away so he could see the ground.

The battle fever raged in him, preparing him to survive this encounter with the unknown as it had so often before. But this time there was no one to fight, no beast to kill. This time he was simply overwhelmed with too many new sounds, sights, scents, and sensations all at once.

He shifted his attention over to the right, where wheeled things moved by with startling speed on a black surface just as flat but not as smooth. Of course the things that moved by were far more interesting than the surface. They were beautiful, made of all the colors of the precious jewels, of different metals and glass, more metal and glass than he'd seen in his whole life or ever hoped to see. What were they? Where were they going? How did they move without horses to pull them? Why did they make so much noise? Were there people inside?

He was so frustrated at not understanding what he was seeing and not knowing what things were!

And there was no place he could rest his eyes. When he glanced away from the people and the strange jeweled objects, there were only brief patches of flowers to look at before his eyes landed on one of the hundreds of buildings that loomed up all around him, blocking the view of the mountains that must surely lie beyond. Every last one of these buildings was ten times as big as Ualraig's castle. How many people must there be here in order to need so many buildings? Where was the person in charge of them? Certies he should be seeing to it they were na so rude!

And the noise! His ears were full of hundreds of noises he didn't recognize or understand. Loud sudden noises and jarring long noises. Sound that resembled music but wasn't made of any instrument he ever heard before. The infernal noise was pervasive, and he didn't understand how everyone was ignoring it.

The place smelled bad too. The most noxious smoke ever lingered in the air, and it stung his eyes.

If all that wasn't enough, then the sight of the oddest trees imaginable pushed Luag over the edge. These trees shot up fifty feet in the air before they had any branches. Their branches were all bunched together in a ball at the top of the tree. They looked like huge skinny one-legged giants with big heads.

The only familiar thing that saved him from insanity was he was still with Katherine. And she looked calm, happy even. Obviously, she had seen all these things before and didn't consider them unusual in the least.

"I need to get back home right away," he told her, surprising himself by speaking fluent English. "This place is extremely unpleasant."

Instead of agreeing with him though, she scowled and groaned her displeasure at what he had said. "Aw,

I finally get home and now I'm stuck with you? Why did you have to come with me?"

He took another look around just to assure himself it really was as odd as he had thought. "Och, this is your home? No wonder you traveled back in time." With all this change, it pleased him that some of the words he said at least were still familiar. Apparently, whatever magic had allowed the lasses to speak Gaelic in his time was also allowing him to speak English in hers, but it left a few colorful words in his speech, and he appreciated that.

Katherine groaned again, and this time it was more like a growl. "What am I going to do with you?"

Chapter Eight

Taran was dizzy, disoriented, and confused. How had he gotten on the ground? Where were Leif and Luag? They had been standing right here a moment ago. There were no threats nearby, so who had tackled him, and why? Negotiations with Donald were going smoothly and according to plan. Prospects looked good. But then, where was Donald?

But all that was in the back of Taran's mind, because the great majority of his consciousness was centered on Lauren. She was holding his face tenderly in her hands, and her own sweet face was inches away from his. Her loving eyes were gazing deeply into his, dripping tears. She was at once both so beautiful and so heartbroken, it made him want to cry as well.

But that wasn't the biggest surprise.

Not by a mile.

Taran could hear Lauren's thoughts! They were as lovely as he always knew they'd be.

"Och! 'Tis so glad I am, tae be here with ye. Ye canna imagine how glad. Ye're alive. Ye're wull. We hae a future together. Aye, I will settle doon with ye in that little cottage by Cresh Manor. I want naught more in all the waurld, and it makes me sae happy tae ken ye want me tae. Let us run away and start this verra moment. Tae heck with all this conflict, and... Nay, ye hae the right o' it, Galdus. Aye, I ken. We hae tae wait for the conflict tae be ower sae that we can get ye the artifact. But promise me Taran survives this. Promise me."

Taran marveled, and then it occurred to him. If he could hear Lauren's thoughts, then could she hear his?

"Lauren," he tested thinking at her, "I canna believe ye are here either. I hae longed tae hold ye this way ever syne I foremaist met ye. Ye mean the waurld tae me. Glad I am that ye want tae bide with me and be my wife."

He could also see what Lauren saw in her mind, and now she saw them together in an idyllic version of Gammer's cottage. Everything was new, from the bed lovingly cut and pegged to the bedding lovingly stitched and stuffed and embroidered to the rugs Lauren had made with love to the dishes the town's women had made and even the furs in the windows, from a special hunting trip the townsmen had taken. The dirty dishes from their private wedding supper sat on the table, and their two chairs had been pulled close together. Their clothing lay gently over the tops of the chairs.

He caressed her face and drew her down toward him for a kiss. And then his vision took over, in their minds. The two of them were in the bed together, cuddled up close after their marital lovemaking, holding each other close and talking late into the night of their future plans.

"I ken ye hae seen much o' the waurld," he said softly next to her ear as their cheeks caressed each other. "Will ye be happy tae stay the rest o' yer life here in Cresh Manor?"

Her arms went more fiercely around him. "So long as you are here with me, I will be more happy here that I could be anywhere else." How soon do you want to start our family?"

He chuckled deep in his throat. "Is not that what we just did?"

She laughed deep in her throat as well. "I suppose it is." And are you glad? As glad as I am, I mean, at the prospect of being a parent?"

He took her face in his hands gently and gave her a kiss that he hoped would show her all the love that he felt for her and for the prospect of starting a family together. "Och aye lass I am happier at that than anything other than making you my bride."

"There is nothing in the world that can make me happier than I am right now except perhaps when our children come and we get to meet them," she said between placing soft kisses on his jaw, his temple, his ear.

"Aye, I never imagined being this happy." He lay back with a smile she continued placing her kisses.

She shook her head a little, which made her hair tickle his face. "I did na either. I cannot believe I am rid of Galdus. I thought I would never be able to touch you so long as we lived, never be free of him."

He gathered her to him and held her tight. "Aye, I feared so as wull."

A mischievous smile spread on her face as she lay there beside him now, her eyes sparkling at him. "Did you truly wish to hold me in your arms the moment you met me?"

"Aye, and even more besides," he said with his own mischievous smile as he traced hers with his fingertip.

Laughing, she grabbed his finger and pulled on it, rolling back so that he landed on top of her, and they enjoyed another time of marital bliss. After they were once more spent and their breathing had returned to its usual pace, they lay there in bed once more, tired but unwilling to go to sleep, unwilling to say goodbye even for the few hours their eyes would be closed and they would be unaware of the world.

"Katherine is far more beautiful than me," Lauren said with a puzzled look on her face even as she caressed his bare chest with her soft hand. "And Jessica is far more feminine, caring and nurturing. Whatever made you want me so, upon first sight?" She made a sage and knowing face. "I mean I know I'm the smartest of the three, but how could you know that before we'd spoken much?" She paused with a sly smile, but he could tell she was eagerly awaiting his response.

Holding her worried gaze with his admiring and loving one, he tried to tell her just how amazed he had been. "Ye kenned the strongest place in Alvin's barn would be in that corner somehow, and ye had just arrived in toon, sae ye didna ken it had caved in there and been rebuilt. Ye couldna hae seen the fresh build for all the hay in the way. Ye also kenned tae rest against the stronger wall, even though the other wall would hae given ye a better view out intae toon, from the other window. Ye kenned aught nay other lass I ever met would ken. Ye still dae, and ye amaze me each day with all ye understand..."

In the way of dreams, especially those one has during the daylight when one is wide-awake, the future soared forward. Taran was awestruck to see Lauren bear him first one son and then another. A daughter came next, and though Taran had always had a soft spot in his heart for his little sister Amena, he now knew that was nothing compared to having his own girl child. He loved the wee lass with a fierceness that he knew there were no bounds to. And with every child he loved Lauren even more.

And Lauren thrived in Inverurie. He needn't have

worried that staying here with him weakened her prospects for the future at all. She created first one wonder and then another in the town, chutes that took the water from the well to houses in the town, and down the hill from Cresh Manor into the fields. She made a machine driven by the mill wheel that wove flax thread into linen. The town sold this cloth and all were prosperous, so much so that extra building materials were acquired and all the houses made warmer and more snug for the winter. Everyone adored Lauren, and along with Taran and Leif and Jessica she was revered as a lady should be.

The prosperity of the town brought growth, and it grew from a town into a veritable city, with market days to rival those of Ualraig's castle. Lauren saw that a school was built for the children, and Father Craig saw that they were taught. He had two apprentices now, and they built a larger church for the town, to accommodate all the people who now lived here. Everyone was happy and well fed and warm in the winter.

But also in the way of dreams dreamt during the day's wakefulness, this one the two of them shared ended abruptly as Taran remembered his current surroundings. Gasping, he grabbed her hand off his face and gently nudged her away. He couldn't get up himself until she moved.

"Ye need tae go, Lauren. These men are na the friendly sort. Make yerself disappear again."

Lauren tugged on his arm, trying to pull him to his

feet. "Come with me, Taran. Galdus, make him invisible too. I did na get sae close tae him just tae lose him in the coming battle."

All that came out of Galdus was a wicked laugh that made Taran shudder.

Abruptly, Lauren was yanked away from Taran's grasp, kicking and screaming.

The man who grabbed her was on horseback, and he pulled her up easy as could be. "We hae what we need right here. Let us be away."

Donald and his two men rode off with her.

Taran was alone.

Chapter Nine

Lauren bounced helplessly, held fast on the back of the horse by her captors.

"Galdus, dae some aught!"

"What can I dae? They hae yer hands held fast. I canna draw myself from the scabbard."

"There are a million things ye could dae, and ye ken it. Go intae their minds and make them crazy. They hae their hands on me, sae I ken ye can get intae their minds. If ye choose tae, ye could let me hear their thoughts."

"Ha! Ye dinna need tae hear," he said with haughtiness. "I am inside their minds, and they hae told me some aught surprising."

"Never mind that, get me away from them!"

"Och, wull even though ye didna ask me what surprising thing I found out, I wull tell ye anyway. I'm feeling generous. Roland, an auld druid friend o' mine, just telt me he wull follow yer friend Katherine home. As soon as my friend finds his way back tae this time, he wull rejoin the Laird o' the Isles. Sae I think 'tis best if we are part o' Laird Donald's party as wull, dinna ye? For Taran and Leif will only return tae that infernal wee toon, but Laird Donald is going across all o' Scotland. Who kens how many artifacts we will encounter in his company? Aye, we shall get the one prophesied from the coming conflict, but oor new plan is tae bide with Laird Donald and get more. I only need ye tae bide with me till Roland returns, tae keep me out o' Laird Donald's hands. The future where he wields me is na pretty for any o' yer friends, sae I ken ye will help. My druid friend was a bit afraid tae go tae Katherine's home, having heard 'twas full o' man-made things that wull sap Nature's power from him. But I assured him Scotland was much the same in yer time, sae how bad could her home be? He wull be back within the span o' days."

Fear for Katherine gripped Lauren.

"If 'tis sae bad for druids there, then why did he want tae go?"

"He didna say, but do you want tae know what I suspect?"

"Nay, but ye will tell me anyway."

Galdus laughed with genuine amusement.

"Fair enough. I suspect 'twas plain curiosity."

Lauren supposed that was better than some evil motive to ruin Katherine's life — perhaps even at Galdus's request.

Galdus's evil laugh confirmed that he could hear her thoughts even when she wasn't thinking directly at him. She had hoped that with practice, she would be able to shield her thoughts from him, but now she doubted that would ever be possible.

Laird Donald's men trotted far too long, jostling her about before they carried her into the castle she'd visited once before, the day Amy came to live with them. Only now Laird Ualraig's castle was inhabited by Laird Donald and his men. Who knew what they had done to Laird Ualraig. She didn't want to think about it. They brought her into an opulent chamber, unceremoniously dumped her on the bed, and then left, closing the heavy door behind them.

Fear and dread gripped her. This did not bode well. She looked to the window for escape. It was an arrow-slit window, and she just might be able to wriggle through. But then what? It was a sheer three-story drop, and when she looked around outside, there was nothing to climb onto.

Inspiration struck.

Hope surged through her as she hastily pulled all the covers off the bed and tied them together corner to corner with as tight of knots as she could manage, wetting them with her mouth and pulling them even tighter so they wouldn't slip. When she was done, she eyed her handiwork with joy. Her improvised rope was plenty long enough to make it all way to the ground, and though someone would likely see her leaving and come over and bring her back here, she had to try.

And then she looked around and deflated.

There wasn't any bed stand to tie the rope to, nor anything else. The door opened with a straight latch. The washstand and wardrobe were heavy oak that sat directly on the stone floor with no feet. They were too heavy for her to even lift a corner.

"Galdus, get me oot o' here! if the laird... has his way with me — even if he just traps me under him — certies he will be able tae reach ye. 'Tis in yer best interest tae get me oot!"

But Galdus's voice came sultry and sickeningly sweet in her mind then, and she knew she was doomed. When you polished off his druidic veneer, he was just a weak man. A pig, like every weak man. Disgusting. And frightening.

"I should love for that laird tae lay his hand on ye while ye yet hae me on ye. That will mean I am privy tae his pleasure. And as for him taking me for his own, dinna fear, my love. I am all yers. I will burn the hand o' anyone who tries tae draw me from this scabbard, while ye keep me near. And ye will keep me near. I shall see tae that. Sae ye hae naught tae fear. Na on my account."

Lauren wasn't sure why she ran to the washstand and used the bowl to catch her vomit. This was the chamber of her enemy, after all. What did she care if it was soiled?

"I dinna care if I'm stranded in this time forever. I'm better off without ye, Galdus!"

She had every intention of detaching Galdus's scabbard from her belt and hurling it out the open window. She even thought she had reached out and grabbed the scabbard.

But her hand still rested on the pitcher of water that sat within her vomit inside the wash bowl. Bile rose in her throat again. Galdus was gaining control of her movements! His evil laughter punctuated the fact that he was pleased about that.

She heard voices coming down the hall, the first one commanding.

"We shall be dining in my quarters by ourselves. See tae it food is brought, and wine. Ye yourselves bide out in the hallway. Nay, bide doon the hallway a discrete distance away, ye ken?"

Raucous laughter came from the men at this.

"Aye, Laird Donald."

"It shall be so, Laird Donald."

"Ye hae only tae state yer wants, Laird."

"She is a braw lass, Laird Donald."

Lauren looked over at her rope of bedclothes, but she didn't see any reason to try and hide what she'd done. Surely he knew she didn't want to be here. Unwilling to look like a cowering victim, she stood up straight right where she was, resisting the urge to move with her back against the wall.

That was all she had time to do before the door opened and a man who was surely Laird Donald entered his chamber — the chamber he had stolen from Laird Ualraig. At first, Donald smiled large at her, but then he noticed the rope and went over to examine it briefly before looking up at her with an admiring smile on his face.

"'Tis verra clever, lass. Whatever stopped ye from using it?"

So long as he was talking, he wasn't having his way with her.

Keep him talking.

Shrugging in a way she hoped was charming—even though it made her sick, the idea of trying to charm this man—she said, "I couldna find anything tae tie it tae."

He threw back his head and laughed, which made her relax the tiniest bit. She'd heard the jokes men made about not being able to ... perform ... if they were amused. Maybe if she confessed to more foolishness, he would laugh some more.

"I was sick a moment ago, and I was na quite sure where tae put it, so 'tis in yer washbasin."

But Donald looked at her with concern, and instead of laughing, he went to the door and opened it, calling out, "Come take away this soiled washbasin, and bring a fresh one before the meal arrives."

Immediately, two of his men came in and did as he said, not wasting any time about it and very carefully not looking at her. They kept their faces to the floor, mumbling obsequiously the whole time.

"As ye will, my Laird."

"I live tae serve, my Laird."

They were gone in no time, and Lauren was alone with Donald once more. Her knees were shaking, but she hoped he didn't notice. She hoped...

Donald went to the door again. "Hurry up with the wine at least, and see what's taking sae long aboot the food." And then he turned to her and smiled apologetically. Apologetically! "Please, have a seat." He gestured not to the bed, but to one of the two chairs at the small breakfast table.

Maybe he's hungry.

Keeping her eyes on the man, she moved past the chair he held out so that the table was between the two of them and sat down with her back against the corner of the room. And instantly realized her mistake. She had cornered herself. She couldn't get away now. There was nowhere to move to. Dread sank into her stomach. It would be infinitely more uncomfortable here against the stone wall than it would've been if she'd sat on the bed.

Had he done that deliberately? Did he like the idea

of her being scraped against the stones, if he took advantage of her?

Bile rose in her throat again. This time she swallowed it down, not wanting to show more weakness than she already had. Resisting the urge to squeeze her eyes closed and hug her knees up to her chest, Lauren forced herself to sit there, calmly watching him.

But he gave her a charming smile and sat down in the chair he had pulled out for her. The look in his eyes was the cunning sort of charm, though. She was not fooled. He was not a gentleman, not this man who had taken over half of Scotland by force, including this very castle whose missing people had welcomed her with warm hospitality only half a year ago.

There was a knock at the door, and she jumped.

"Come," was all the Laird said. He did so without even looking at the door. His eyes were drinking her in.

Which made her even more afraid. She knew it was meant to be a compliment, but ... She was glad he wasn't very good at being charming. Better the enemy you know than the one you think is a friend.

A parade of men came in with not only their wine and wine glasses, but also two plates of food and eating utensils. They arranged it all on the table quickly and left even more quickly, softly closing the door behind them. She could hear their footsteps scuttling down the hall, but no voices at all. She got the feeling they obeyed out of fear of punishment, rather than out of love for their laird, as the people of Inverurie obeyed Leif.

Smiling his fake charming smile, Donald poured wine for them and held his other hand out toward her plate. "Please, refresh yerself. These men I travel with are clumsy and wanting in the social graces, but the food was prepared by the original cooks from the castle, and they are quite skilled. Ye will like the food. Please eat."

It was on the tip of her tongue to refuse. The tale of the woman who went down to the underworld and had to stay there six months because she ate six pomegranate seeds popped into her mind. Persephone?

But Lauren didn't refuse, because so long as they were eating. they weren't... She took up the knife and started cutting her meat. She didn't know what type of meat it was, but it did smell good.

"My," said Laird Donald, "I kenned yer ways would be different, but I had na idea just how different. Does everyone from the future eat that way?"

Lauren's stomach lurched. She covered it up by taking a sip of her wine. "I'm sure I dinna ken what ye mean."

Laird Donald chuckled and took a sip of his own wine. He had impeccable table manners, not getting any wine on his lip and not making any noise when he set down his glass. "'Tis a lovely bracelet ye wear," he said, nonchalantly changing the subject.

Quickly, Galdus cut into her thoughts. "He is

fishing for the object ye use tae time travel. Go ahead and play up that 'tis yer bracelet. That suits our purpose perfectly. He must na ken that 'tis... me."

Unable to resist some sarcasm, Lauren told Galdus, "Now ye decide tae be o' use tae me."

Galdus rewarded her with his amused laughter, but it didn't settle her stomach. She was still all alone in this, one woman against at least two men, if not a castle full. Her only hope was that maybe Laird Donald's only interest in her was in obtaining her time travel implement. This hope welled up in her bosom. She did her best to fight it, dreading the letdown should it prove false.

"Play up the bracelet," Galdus urged again, cutting through her thoughts.

Oh yeah.

"Och," she said, playing with the thin band of gold on her wrist, "this is just something my parents gave me when I finished school."

When she said she had been to school, Donald choked on his wine and even dribbled some, but he recovered quickly, saying "It looks quite valuable."

She hid it under the table. "It has sentimental value, is all."

"'Twas the truth, yet ye delivered it wull," Galdus marveled.

She ignored him. He had made it clear he only had his own interests in mind and would betray hers at his first opportunity.

"So how does it work?" The Laird asked ever so nonchalantly, clarifying without need, "Time travel."

Lauren carefully took another sip of her wine. How much to tell him? "'Tis naught I often talk aboot, ye ken."

He nodded, holding her gaze steadfastly. He wasn't going to give up until she answered him.

And why shouldn't I? What's the harm, really?

"There is na harm," Galdus assured her, "sae long as he doesna ken 'tis me ye speak aboot. And even then, I am na gae' na let him get hold o' me."

The laird raised his eyebrows, amused at her hesitation.

Lauren took a deep breath and steeled herself, trying to tamp down the nervousness. "Time travel can work anywhere, but 'tis easier if ye go tae a sacred grove or some other place the druids hae made special. My friend's husband has an implement that only works in one location, but other implements can work anywhere and take ye tae any place in any time. Really, it depends on the druid who designed it." She took another bite, glancing at him in what she hoped was a way that seemed incidental, but really trying to gauge if he was satisfied with her answer or not.

But of course he wasn't. Why would he be satisfied with that when he had her literally captive? No, he settled in. She had the feeling this is only the beginning. But then again so long as he was talking...

"And how was it ye were chosen, tae hae such a powerful tool?"

Despite herself, Lauren smiled at that. "It depends who ye ask. Dae ye want the long story, or the short story?"

He gave her another genuine smile. It made him actually look handsome for just a moment, before she remembered she was his captive and he was the cruel overlord over half of Scotland now, having taken all by force.

"Why the long story, o' course," he said. "I hae nowhere tae go until tomorrow's battle. Aye, I dae need a little sleep before that, but the day is young yet. I hae plenty o' time tae listen." And again in his fake charming way, he settled his chin on top of his hand with his elbow resting on the table in a near perfect imitation of a young schoolboy listening to a teacher.

Lauren allowed her memories to take her away from the horrible circumstances as she told him her tale. "My friend's husband who I mentioned before?"

He nodded. "Aye."

"Wull, he's a MacGregor—"

"Aye? Fierce warriors, indeed. I could use him on my campaign here... Aha, but he is na here in this time, is he? Nay, he is someone ye met in the future where ye come from." He smiled his genuine smile, a frightening smile. The smile of a hunter who has spotted his prey.

Keep him talking, Lauren.

She took a deep breath and rushed on with her story, trying to make it as good as she could. "Aye, he is someone I met in the future. His father belongs tae a long line o' MacGregors who were cursed by a druid generations afore his. Their ancestor was a gambler, ye see—"

Donald interrupted her. "And sure I am that is a charming tale as well. Howsoever, let us get back tae the way ye were chosen by the druids tae travel time for them. If ye please." There was that fake charm again, accompanied by an 'if you please' sliding hand gesture that should have been gentlemanly but wasn't.

"Verra wull," she said, willing her heart to stop thumping so loud. "Tavish's father Dall belonged to this sub clan of the MacGregors. He was from the 1540s, which is still the future to you, but you see I am from the 2000's. Dall and his son were from 500 years before my time. The druid who enslaved their clan sent them forward because we romanticize your time. We have what they call Renaissance Faire, where we reenact history. Anyhow, Dall was sent forward to help the Renaissance Faire be authentic. He taught Gaelic and dancing and sword fighting. He met his wife there and took her back to his time and they had many adventures together. They still talk about him in my time as the man who brought kilts to the faire—"

Donald reached toward where Lauren's hand rested on the table, and she hastily withdrew, gasping in fear. He raised his hands up a mock surrender,. "Ye would na be telling me a tall tale tae avoid admitting how ye were chosen, would ye?"

Lauren caught her breath and put her hand on her chest to help calm herself.

"Nay. 'Tis all part o' that tale. Dall and Emily had two sons, and his son Peadar had four sons. Dall and Emily's youngest son Tavish and Vange's youngest son John were both beholden as slaves tae the druids. But the boys didna ken this when they were bairns. By tradition, their parents allowed them normal childhoods and didna tell them till the oldest was eighteen years auld and might marry. Sae all the MacGregor lads took up with lasses. We had glorious times together, we six lasses and the six lads.

"And then Dall and Peadar telt their sons about the curse. Only nay one telt us lasses. The lads just disappeared from oor lives with nary telling us naught. Betimes we thought they were dead. Only a year hence did we reconnect, and that started a chain o' events that brought the rest o' us back intae contact with the MacGregor clan, and in one way or another we hae all been chosen.

"I telt ye it depended who ye asked. Some o' us lasses think we were chosen when we were thirteen. Others believe we are only now being chosen, that the seven years we didna hear from them was some sort o' test o' loyalty. Either way, the result is the same. We six lasses were chosen by the druids tae travel through time."

Donald opened his mouth to speak, staring at her bracelet.

But she interrupted him this time. "And afore ye think tae just take the bracelet from me, ken 'tis bonded with me. 'Twill burn whoever touches it."

At this, Laird Donald made a show of looking deflated.

But Lauren knew he was only biding his time until his druid Roland returned. Little did the laird know.

Chapter Ten

Taran ran after the horse over the tall grass of the battlefield as fast as he could, yelling at the top of his lungs without a care who heard him or followed. "Lauren! Lauren, dinna lose hope! I will get ye away from him, Lauren!"

A hand landed on Taran's shoulder, and he turned with his sword still in his hand, ready to hack down the enemy who tried to stop him from rescuing her.

But it was Leif, and his brother looked mystified and troubled. "Taran, one moment ye were there with me, listening tae the earl negotiate with Laird Donald, and the next moment, ye were gone."

Taran grasped his brother's shoulder as well, clutching it with the urgency he felt.

"Never ye mind that. Laird Donald and his men hae taken Lauren captive! I must go and get her away from them!" He tried to shrug off Leif's grip.

But Leif held on tight. "Taran, ye canna go now. Dinna waste what wee amount o' time we hae gained from the negotiations. Oor men need us. Allow oor reinforcements tae arrive this evening. Luag is nowhere tae be found. I feared ye both were dead. Ye and I are all there is tae see that the men o' Inverurie prepare themselves well for the morrow's battle."

Taran struggled with Leif, but his brother was stronger.

"Nay, I dinna care. I must get tae her afore Laird Donald... afore he hurts her beyond repair. He is a cruel man, Leif. Ye ken that, aye? I love her, Leif." A horrible thought occurred to Taran. "Jessica was here, tae! They may hae taken her captive as wull. They—"

"Nay," Leif told him with reassurance on his face. "I was amazed tae hear word that she had arrived in oor camp, but I hae assurances that she is wull. Taran, I understand ye want tae go, but ye must bide here for the battle. If ye dinna, we may lose. Donald has too many men. If ye leave and dae get her back, there may be naught tae return tae."

Taran still struggled. "I remind ye, she is under oor protection."

Leif loosened his hold, and then let go. "I ken ye mean tae get in through the tunnel. I agree that is wise. Donald likely does na ken about the tunnel, na yet. Howsoever, ye must bide yer time till dark. If ye go now, someone might see ye go in. Ye would betray the secret and destroy oor advantage for when we take back the castle after we win the battle tomorrow. Bide till dark, use the passageways tae remain unseen, and aye, steal her away with nary anyone being the wiser. The militia will be back that way after the battle, tae take back Ualraig's place."

Taran studied his brother's face. It was sincere, and worried. And he trusted Leif.

"Verra wull. I will return tae camp with ye now, and then under cover o' darkness, I will gae and get my lass."

Chapter Eleven

A man came and lit Donald's hearth fire, but the July evening was quite warm, so the window was still undressed.

Lauren glanced outside and felt oppressed by the darkness that had crept up on her while her eyes adjusted to the candlelight inside. Shivering despite the warmth of the fire, she took the last bite of food from her second meal here, then leaned back in her seat and sighed with just a bit of pleasure. Not too much. She was, after all, a captive. Just enough to show that she did feel less apprehensive with all that Laird Donald had promised her.

He would sleep in the next chamber. He only wanted her time travel tool, and his druid would be able to get it detached from her without injury. She needn't fear.

That suited her just fine, no matter if the druid

gave Galdus to Donald or not. Lauren could count on Kelsey to find a way for her to get home — if she wanted to go home. This brought thoughts of Taran, and she lost focus for a moment in a daydream of the two of them at the cottage...

"Dae ye grow sleepy already?" Laird Donald asked with amusement. "I ken these summer nights are warm, and the fire is just a precaution, na really needed it all, howsoever 'tis hardly time tae retire. I hae a battle ahead o' me on the morrow. Pray, keep me company late intae the evening."

Lauren was collecting her thoughts, trying to figure out what to say, when she had to stifle a gasp. Taran was nearby! He was within ten feet of her, because she could hear his thoughts. He was determined, focused, and frantic.

"She's right there on the other side o' this wall! That's her voice I hear through the cracks. The door willna budge. I need tae shove it open!"

"Dinna!" Lauren screamed at Taran in her mind. "Donald is here with me! Dinna get yerself captured as wull, Taran! They would kill ye. I could na bear that! Once Donald goes tae sleep, I will meet ye at the door doon the row, the one at the nursery."

Donald was starting to get up to help her out of her seat.

She shuddered. She wouldn't let him touch her if she could help it.

"Nay," the laird said to her without hiding his

disappointment. "'Tis not time for bed yet, but if ye insist, then let me help ye." He held up his hand help-fully for her to take in order to support her presumably sleepy self.

Lauren pulled away from him, sitting up straight against the hard stone corner of the room. Was this it after all, the moment when he threw aside all pretense at civility? The moment she would be crushed against the cold stone wall?

"Nay," she said with the kind of feminine hand dip she despised, even in movies, making her voice sound playful and maybe just a tiny bit flirtatious. She had to keep Donald talking. He was interested in the details of time travel, so perhaps if she kept on that leg of their conversation he would back off and sit down and listen again. She had to try. "Nay, I am na sleepy yet—"

But Lauren was rendered speechless by the anguish in Taran's response.

"She's enjoying herself with him! Would she even welcome me if I found my way intae their chamber? It doesna sound like it. Hae I misread her? I was sae sure she loved me! Nay. She does love me. There was nae way I could hae misunderstood the lass's verra thoughts. But I dinna ken her at all if she is sae simple as tae be lured away from a love such as oors by the prospect o' being the lady o' a castle. Nay. Listen awhile longer, Taran. Ye must be mistaken. Ye hae tae be mistaken. 'Tis unbearable otherwise."

"Taran!" Lauren thought with all her might at the

man she loved. "Taran, I just dae what I must in order tae get along. Once free I am from here, we will go tae oor cottage together for the rest o' oor lives. I just need tae bide here till Galdus's druid comes back. Then I wull be free—"

"If ye are certain 'tis not yet time for bed," Donald said with that fake charming smile, "then pray tell me more. Tell me aboot the future."

"Bed!" Taran thought.

Lauren screamed at Taran in her mind, "No! I only humor him! You are the only one I want, Taran!"

But mystifyingly, Taran argued, "Nay. Ye are wrong. She would na."

"That's right, Taran! I would na!" Lauren called out to Taran mentally, plagued by his anguish though confused by his words. But she didn't have the luxury of thinking through Taran's words right now.

She had to deal with Donald, who sat in front of her. Relieved to see the laird was no longer reaching out to touch her, she used her fingers to comb out her hair as an excuse to keep them off the table. "Wull nae," she said aloud to Donald, "the biggest difference between yer time and the future I live in is the advances in engineering."

But even as she spoke, realization hit her. Even though she knew it was futile, she desperately called out in her mind to Taran, "Dinna believe a word Galdus tells ye, Taran! He is a liar and a deceiver! I only pretend tae be the laird's friend, Taran! Only tae pacify him till I can make my escape! I pray ye ignore what yer ears hear and listen tae me with yer heart, Taran! "

Meanwhile, she had to concentrate to remember what Laird Donald had just said... Oh yeah. He had said, "Dae tell me about yer engineering advances."

But she was still listening in her mind for Taran to tell her of course he knew she was true to him, and for him to confirm her plan to meet with him at the nursery entrance to the secret passageway later.

But all she heard from Taran were vague anguished rumblings.

And Galdus was giggling like a schoolgirl.

Oh! Donald still awaited her reply! She mustn't ignore him. There were limits to what a prisoner could get away with, after all.

She rattled off to Donald the first thing that came to mind when considering the state of engineering in the Middle Ages. "In my time, we hae taken the mill and built on it, ye ken? It can dae more than grind grain."

"Aye?" Donald said with interest, his eyes full of possibilities and amazement — the latter at having this conversation with a woman.

She stopped herself just in time from rolling her eyes. Even some modern men reacted that way to her and other female engineers. She was sick and tired of it.

"Aye," he said again, "now that ye mention it, I can see how a windmill might draw water, perchance..."

'Wow,' Lauren thought to herself, 'Donald isn't as stupid as he ... No. He isn't stupid in any way, just vapid. Keep your wits about you.'

She still called out to Taran in her mind, knowing Galdus was not passing her thoughts along, but at a loss for how else to reach him. "Taran? Did ye hear me? I will meet ye in the nursery after Donald goes tae sleep."

To Donald, she said, "Aye, windmills can and dae draw water."

Laird Donald raised his eyebrows artfully. "What other wondrous work does the mill dae in yer future?"

Growing more and more desperate for Taran's answer, Lauren again spoke to Donald by rote, reciting answers she remembered from freshman engineering class, albeit in Gaelic. "We hae indeed harnessed engines tae draw water, and we hae tubes made o' metal that stretch doon intae the ground below the house and from there tae a lake or river. Aye, vast expanses o' metal tubing called pipes..."

Meanwhile, she kept searching for the thoughts of her love. "Taran? Taran, tell me ye hear me! Tell me ye will meet me this evening!"

Was Galdus blocking her from hearing Taran now as well? A part of her wished she had never set eyes on the dagger! But then she would never have met the man she loved. The man Galdus was driving away from her, now that the ancient druid had found people who served his purpose better.

It was all she could do to keep her face free of the sickness that was creeping into her stomach. Still searching for Taran's answer in her mind, hoping for it, yearning for it, she rattled off the closest things she could think of, to keep Donald occupied with plans for time travel.

"And we hae complex engines tae drive the water tae each and every house. The work that drives the water comes from even more complex engines that take the work o' running water and convert it intae energy we can transmit ower vast distances using verra thin stretches o' metal called wires..."

She didn't think Donald was faking his fascination any longer. As she spoke, his face grew more and more animated with astonishment until now his jaw was just about on the floor. It would be amusing if not for Taran's pain.

Anger bloomed in Lauren. "Galdus, ye stop lying tae Taran and let him hear me, and ye dae it right now!"

Galdus's giddy laughter filled her mind before the ancient druid guffawed, "Or what, my love?"

"Or I wull throw you intae this fire is what!"

His laughter reached a crescendo. "Try tae. Gae on."

She would do better than try! She reached for the handle of the jagged dagger sheathed at her waist and—

And her hand was still combing through her hair! Galdus had gained control of her hand!

She tried to reach for him with her other hand, straining to grab the dagger and throw it into the fire, where she envisioned it turning red hot and then melting away to vapor...

And her other hand still rested on the arm of her chair.

Donald caught her attention by swiftly leaning back in his chair with a faraway look in his eyes while saying, "My, the things ye hae seen, the knowledge ye must hae!" His eyes regained their focus and he looked at her with a new appreciation, not for her experience at time travel this time, but for her brains. "And if I gave ye the stone and the metal, and command o' enough men, could ye make any o' these wonders come tae be now, in my time?"

Now he was speaking her language, and for once, talking to him wasn't excruciatingly awkward. "I hae already done some o' it, in Inverurie. Water closets and some rudimentary irrigation. 'Tis the sort o' thing I enjoy doing."

And then Lauren's breath caught midway through her exhale. What could she say to Donald that would really be to Taran? What would allay her love's fears? Inspiration struck.

"But o' course," she said, "as soon as yer druid comes back, he will take ye tae the future. Ye will see all these things for yerself. Ye dinna need me, just the bracelet." For Donald's sake, she batted her eyelashes, though it made her throw up a little in her mouth.

"Nay," Donald said, but his eyes were far away again, then back at her, then far away again. "Nay, I willna need ye then. Sae tell me, how are these long tubes o' metal for water made? In a smithy?"

Again, he was speaking her language. She warmed to the subject despite herself. "In a way, yes, but the smithies are huge in my time. They employ thousands o' people and take up more land than ten o' these castles."

One advantage Lauren had was that the Laird o' the Isles spent so much energy exuding his fake charm that he didn't appear to notice hers. He still was taken in by their conversation, asking her, "Hae ye been tae times that I might hae heard about in history, then?"

Putting on her best charming smile, she answered, "Aye. I hae been tae the time when the people who rule this land fought off the Romans, who sought tae take it ower." Even as she smiled at Donald and courted his distraction, she let herself hope that perhaps Taran had heard her despite what Galdus said. Perhaps her love would meet her at the nursery door this evening, once Donald slept.

Again, Donald appeared impressed and surprised. Excitement shone in his eyes before he once again schooled his face to that fake charming one. "Aye? And that was the time o' the druids as wull, was na? Tae my way o' thinking, ye Lauren must hae seen some astonishing feats."

Lauren gave him a self-effacing smile, and looked down to her hands folded in her lap. "Nay. Nay, I was there but for an afternoon. I did see the inside o' a living broch, but nay, 'tis my friend Jaelle who still lives there and has made a life there. She has seen wonders beyond what either o' us would believe. She married a Pictish chieftain o' ten clans."

Again Donald rested his chin on his hand in that boyishly charming way of his, looking up at her with beseeching eyes. But she saw through him. He only wanted the information, and he didn't even mean to credit her with any of it. When he spoke, it was in that sickeningly sweet tone that was making her nauseous. "Surely this Jaelle has told ye some o' the feats she has seen..."

❧

At long last, Donald got up and collected his sword and shield, as well as the bow he had set down beside the door, then turned to leave her chamber.

"I would keep company with ye and hear these tales all the night long, lass, but I hae a battle tae attend on the morrow. Sae I must leave ye in order tae get my rest. My men are doon the hall, sae dinna think o' trying tae leave, although if ye dae wish tae come intae my chamber, ye would be welcome there." He gave her what he assumed to be a charming wink.

Finally, the Laird o' the Isles was gone.

Now she had only to wait for him to be asleep. To pass the time, she looked in all the pouches she had concealed under her leine. Checked to make sure everything was there and in place. Took inventory, as it were. She hadn't known just what she would need, and so she had brought all manner of things: sewing kit, first-aid kit, fabric repair kit, level, screwdriver, safety pins, energy bars, iodine tablets... Just the normal things you brought when you went camping.

Doubt crept into her mind. How would she know when Donald was asleep? She didn't know whether the man snored or not. She would just have to take a chance and assume he slept. She'd better wait a little longer.

It wouldn't be a bad idea to put her feet up for a while and rest. Briefly, she considered undoing the knots that tied the covers together so she could make the bed. Nah. She would just lie down on the bare feather mattress and relax for a bit.

Finally, she saw no reason to put it off any longer and resolved to get up and go in the next room, find the secret door going to the tunnels, and see if Taran was waiting for her at the nursery door.

She crept over to her door, listened at it, heard nothing, and carefully cracked it open. Peeking out into the hallway, she saw that Donald had indeed left men at the other end, near the rest of the castle. Accustomed to modern movies, she expected to see them smoking, but of course they were only standing around, three of them, talking in low tones. They had torches burning down there, but the area in front of her door was mercifully dark. And one advantage of cold stone floors was they didn't creak.

But Donald's chamber door was another story. It creaked when she pushed it open, sending her heart racing.

She ducked back out into the hallway, looking for a shadow she could hide in. All she could do was flatten her back against the wall behind the door and hope Donald's guards didn't come down the hall to investigate. Her breathing came shallow and fast as she waited to hear the footsteps running down the hall — or worse yet, to hear Donald getting up from his bed to come greet her. She waited what seemed like an eternity, but gradually, she relaxed. No one was coming.

Wiping the sweat from her brow with one of her billowing leine sleeves, she went down into a crouch so that anyone looking for her head wouldn't see anything, and she crept into Donald's chamber. And despaired.

Someone had re-arranged the room. The bed was now in the alcove, which made sense. It looked better there. But that meant the heavy wardrobe chest now blocked the door to the secret passageway.

She kept looking at the door, thinking perhaps there was a way she could move the wardrobe.

Donald snorted and rolled over.

Her panicked mind screamed at her, 'Get out of his room, Lauren!'

Anguished, she made herself retrace her steps.

Chapter Twelve

T aran ran the whole way out the tunnel. By the time he was under the stars, he was furiously using the backs of his hands to wipe tears from his eyes for the first time since he'd been considered old enough to wield weapons. His parents had been devoted to each other until the very end, when they had succumbed to the fever which took their lives. They had looked at each other in love every day and done each other small favors: rubbing a shoulder, keeping a seat warm.

Taran wanted more than anything to share that same sort of life with Lauren, in his gammer's cottage. Lauren's thoughts had told him she was anticipating that sort of future together as well, not half a day ago. That vision of their future life together had been so beautiful, and so real.

And then he was there in that future, holding her

in the soft bed. Feeling her caress him. Knowing she loved him every bit as much as he loved her. It felt every bit as real in his memory is it had when they thought it all up together. Her kisses felt real and her caresses. Here in his memory, their love was real. He didn't doubt it for a moment.

He hadn't realized until now that he'd been thinking of their marriage as already accomplished. As a future they had together for certain, not just something they imagined together in those few moments when her hands had held his face.

And why had all that gone out the window? Because the enemy had taken Laird Ualraig's castle. It wasn't even Donald's castle! The cursed man had just taken it.

Taran was now running back to the militia's camp, but he slowed down, because there were tears streaming down his face and sobs wracking his chest.

The fires of Hell would turn to ice before he let anyone see him thus, so he headed down the ravine instead of back to camp. He didn't have time for this senseless mourning over a woman who didn't deserve it. He needed to get her out of his mind and his heart and get back to his duty. The town needed every warrior out there on the field, defending it. His brother needed his help getting the men ready for battle, especially since Luag had disappeared.

Lauren had wasted his entire evening, an evening he should have been with the militia, doing his duty.

For that, she deserved his anger, not his mourning. That's right, he was angry. Good. Anger was familiar. Much safer than tears. Anger, he could deal with.

Jared was the guard on duty where Taran entered camp, and when he saw Taran's face he fell in step beside him, putting an arm over his shoulders. "Has the fighting started already? Who died?"

Taran shrugged it off. "Nay, 'tis only me being weak, and now I put an end tae that. Take me tae my brother. Let us get ourselves ready for battle."

From the look on his face, Jared knew he wasn't getting the whole story, but he was a good man. He didn't pry, and soon they reached the rest of the militia.

Jessica was indeed there with Leif. The two of them stood arm-in-arm addressing the men together, enjoying the sort of love that he and Lauren... No.

False memories kept coming to his mind unbidden. The feel of Lauren's sweet kiss on his lips, his cheek, his shoulder, his neck. The euphoric feeling of having her in his arms and his bed. Her eyes gazing at him in love and respect and admiration.

Taran Had to fight each memory tooth and nail to get it to leave his mind. He would no longer allow himself to think about the lass who had foolishly scorned him. It was her loss, not his.

But he did need to tell his brother Lauren had taken up residence with the enemy. He rushed over, meeting Leif's eyes when he was halfway there.

His brother's face fell when he looked around

Taran and didn't find what he was looking for — Lauren. He started to say something with that fallen face.

But Taran gave his brother a hard look.

Leif stopped, composed himself, and said something else. "We will get her tomorrow, just as I promised."

But Jessica was new to ladyhood. She didn't have the self-control Leif had, not yet. Perhaps not ever. She was the type of lass who felt things deeply, who had a big heart. When Jessica saw Taran returning without her longtime friend, she sank down to the ground on her knees and wailed as if her friend had died.

Taran's heart went out to Jessica, but she was in good hands.

Leif signaled for the men to disperse to their campsites. Once he was sure they were no longer watching the spectacle, he crouched down and held his wife close, then raised her up to stand with him again, patting her back and stroking her hair, soothing her just as Father would have soothed Mother.

Taran couldn't watch. He turned his head away. "'Tis even worse than me failing tae get her. She has decided tae stay with the Laird o' the Isles. She's helping them, thinking even now o' improvements Donald can make tae Ualraig's castle."

Just as he had on the way here, Taran was making himself feel anger instead of sadness. It made him feel far more manly. Clenching his fists, he reveled in the sound of anger in his voice, how strong it was.

But when Jessica heard the anger in his voice, she broke away from Leif and put on her own sort of anger, storming at Taran with her teeth bared and her hands clawed at her sides. "My friend Lauren would never go over tae the enemy! Never, dae ye hear me? Ye hae failed her! She was counting on ye tae rescue her, and ye hae failed her! How could ye give up sae easily, let alone accuse her o' some aught she would never dae!"

Leif ran in front of his wife and grabbed her, holding her back to keep her from advancing on Taran. He sided with his wife in this, and Taran wasn't surprised. But Leif spoke in sadness rather than anger. "Taran, she has the right o' it." He hugged Jessica close to him, and she broke down into sobs again. He turned and called out to the men in their campsites, "Negotiation is na working. We battle tomorrow. All that remains tae do now is get what sleep ye can. Awake at first light, take up weapons, and be ready. After we trounce the invaders, then we take back Ualraig's castle!"

The men cheered at this, and everyone but Taran went to bed in high spirits.

Taran hardly slept a wink that night. He tossed and he turned, telling himself he was angry at Lauren but knowing deep down that she had broken his heart. He had to think of defending Amena before he found the strength inside to go on with the battle.

❦

"WHAT DAE YE MEAN WE GO UP THE HILL?" TARAN asked Leif the next morning as they walked in the direction of the hill between the battlefield and Inverurie. "The earl telt us tae take the field back here."

The rest of the militia was with them, along with Ualraig's few surviving men, who had joined their camp in the middle of the night. Leif looked at the men behind them and smiled conspiratorially, first at them and then at Taran. "Nay, the earl did say tae fortify this area for the retreat back tae Inverurie, and that is what we are doing."

It was true. They were fortifying the area. "Then why am I almost certain he telt us tae stand in this area o' the field?" Taran asked Leif, but the conspiratorial smile was beginning to spread on his own face as well, and he welcomed the feeling of outsmarting their orders. Anything pleasant to think about was a good distraction from... Never mind what from.

"It may be ye hae the right o' it," Leif acknowledged with a slight bow of the head while his conspiratorial smile grew. "Alasdair may hae telt us tae stand here in the field. But the spirit o' what he telt us, I hae na changed. And ye ken as wull as I that we can guard the retreat better on the hill. Why we fight in the field is beyond me."

Taran Looked appreciatively up the steep hill. It had plenty of rocks to hide behind, enough for all the men to be well hidden. He shared a smile with the militiamen before turning back to his brother with a wry grin. "I always thought we fought on fields so that the lairds could show off their knights. Why train such bonnie knights if ye canna use them, aye?"

Leif laughed, as did the rest of the men. "Aye, ye make a verra good point."

But that was the end of fun and games. They took up defensive positions on the mountain, the battle started, and they used up most of their arrows taking out who of the Isles forces they could before the Viking Gaels and the Picts Gaels started slaughtering each other on that field.

It was a gruesome battle with more casualties than Taran had ever heard of in any other. Alasdair had fifteen hundred knights in chainmail, but Donald had thousands and thousands of men. They kept coming, wave after wave, seeming endless.

"Looks like 'tis time for the knights tae go doon and slaughter them on their side o' the field," Taran told Leif with a disgusted shake of his head.

"Aye, Leif agreed. "And the sooner they dae, the sooner everyone can save the wounded. This is a disgusting battle, and I feel nay honor at having been involved in it."

"The honor is all ours," Jared piped up from behind them. "We but defend our own lands."

Leif nodded to Jared with a sad shake of his head. "Aye. Aye, 'tis true."

The knights went down, but wave upon wave of fresh pikers drove them back and back and back again, until at sundown the militia retreated to their edge of the battlefield and lay down to an uneasy sleep in shifts, certain the fighting would resume at first light.

Chapter Thirteen

L auren knew she was dreaming something completely fabricated from her wishful mind, compiled from bits and pieces of this past year's memories, but she enjoyed the time with Taran nonetheless. In her dream, she and Taran were in their cottage, and they were married. They sat arm-in-arm by the fire in the evening, smiling up into each other's eyes as they shared kisses and caresses. It was perfect, like she'd always wanted without even realizing.

"Sae Senga has been here ever syne ye can remember?"

"Aye, as if she were my second mother."

"I wager she could tell some funny stories if I asked her."

He laughed. "O' that I hae nay doubt. But ye could save her the time and ask me instead. She is fearsome busy cooking for nine people now instead o' only four, ye ken."

Lauren chuckled. "That frightened ye are, o' what she might say, eh?"

He put a guilty look on his face. "Ye hae nay idea."

They shared a laugh.

"Verra wull then. What is the funniest story ye can think o' tae tell me, about when ye and Leif were children?"

He caressed her shoulder while he leaned his head back and stared up at the ceiling of the tiny cottage which, now that she looked at it, was interesting, with the shadows from the fireplace dancing on it.

"Aye, well that would hae tae be the time we decided the great room o' the manor house was the best place tae play at war. With mud balls."

She grabbed onto his shoulders and leaned forward, she was laughing so hard. "With mud balls?"

At first his voice sounded wistful behind her, so that for a moment she was sorry she had brought up a memory that made him think of his dearly departed mother. But the more he spoke of this memory, the more amused he sounded, until by the end he was laughing right along with her.

"It wasna only me and Leif. All o' the children from toon were up here with us. Mother had gone doon tae fighter practice with Father that day, and as usual we all ran aroond loose. Ye hae seen how 'tis."

"Aye, and more than one time I hae feared the children would get intae mischief."

He smiled sheepishly. "Well after the mud fight incident in mother's house, we were all chastened pretty well. But you have the right of it. It's been long enough now that we really should have a word with the children. Or at least watch them better."

She gave him a playful shove. "No changing the subject! Tell me about this mud fight in the great hall of Cresh Manor. How old were you?"

Taran shook his head and rolled his eyes at himself, still wearing that sheepish grin. "We were plenty old enough to know better. Leif was ten and I was eight." He snickered. "Jared was fourteen! But it wasn't his mother's house." He hung his head dramatically, tipping his head up sideways to make sure she was appreciating the show he was putting on.

She held her hands up and shook her head at him with a big smile on her face, then rolled one of her hands with palm up to tell him "Get on with it!"

It was getting fun though, because when he continued, the look on his face was amused instead of chagrined. "'Twas a roaring good time. Oor side turned the supper table and hid behind it. Their side built a wall o' the large chairs near the fire and hid behind that. We launched the mud balls at each other. They went out the back door tae get more mud, and we went out the front. 'Twas raining, sae there was plenty o' mud about, and can ye blame us for na wanting tae be outside in the rain?"

Lauren hugged Taran and laughed so hard her nose ran. Wiping it with the back of her hand, she kept laughing, as did he. It felt so good to hold each other and laugh together. They kept at this for several minutes, gradually relaxing back into their chairs to gaze at the fire, every once in a while bursting into giggles anew.

"Sae I'm guessing Senga found ye there with yer mess, and na yer mother."

Taran put his hand on his forehead and leaned down to show embarrassment, but he was still grinning. "Aye, that she did. And 'tis the reason ye still see me before ye, a living soul and na a dead one. Senga put us all tae work cleaning up, and by the time Father and Mother came back from toon, the room was presentable, if na back tae the way it had been. Father left Mother and Senga there tae supervise us while he went doon and got the rest o' the parents, and we all got a talking tae—"

Lauren slapped his upper arm with the back of her hand. "Ye got more than a talking tae. Come now. If my bairns wrecked my living room, I would tan their hides."

Taran pulled his chin in abruptly, showing that he was taken aback. "Would ye now?"

Laughing, she looked him in the eye teasingly. "Nay, I would get ye tae do it!"

JANE STAIN

He nodded once solemnly, but the very corners of his mouth were turned up around his pursed lips. "Aye, and that is just what Mother did. Neither Leif nor I could sit down for days. What were ye like as a child?" He asked her as they both watched the flames climb over the logs. "Did ye use yer engineering talent tae build fortifications out in the field tae defend yerself from the other children ye played war with?"

She squeezed his hand as a laugh escaped her nose, making her wince with embarrassment even as he squeezed her hand back, laughing with her. "Hardly!" she said as if it were preposterous. But it made her think, and when next she spoke her words were considered. "Though now ye say it, I realize even though men and lasses hae equal opportunities in my time, lasses and boys play separately more, compared tae how they play today. Neither I nor any o' my female contemporaries played war with the boys. We lasses played tamer games together, running games and hiding games and ball games. But if the boys did play war, the lasses would all sit and talk and watch them, mayhap, or mayhap we would play hopscotch or jump rope."

He squeezed all of her with all of him, making pleasure shoot through her whole body. "Well then, when did ye ken ye wanted tae study the way aught works?"

She relaxed in his arms, letting her head rest on his shoulder as his strength supported her easily, naturally accommodating her. "Oh, I always knew that. But I hae never been aggressive, not even in play. Studying the way things work is more female than male, in my way o' thinking."

He chuckled. "Och lass, how dae ye reckon that?"

"Creating new things is like childbearing. Destroying things is like battle," she said playfully, knowing she was egging him on.

He put his mouth right next to her ear and breathed out warm air, then chuckled as she shuddered with the chills that ran through her body. "Aye? Methinks it takes two tae create. Shall I show ye?"

And he did.

When Lauren opened her eyes, shivering a bit from the morning chill, for a few moments she wasn't sure where she was. The gray stone walls lit by an open window full of morning light weren't ringing any bells. But when she rolled to the edge of the bed and saw on the floor her rope made of tied bedclothes, she remembered, jumping up off the bed. She was Donald's prisoner in the castle he had stolen from Ualraig.

Lack of the usual sounds of men laughing and joking with each other told her the Isles forces had already left for the battle.

Good.

Having slept in her clothes, she had nothing to do but check to make sure everything was there — not as she could do anything about it if it wasn't, but it would be better to know ahead of time. But everything was there. Nothing was missing. She still had her tape measure and her level, even her slide rule.

If anyone asks you where you're going, just tell them you're looking for breakfast.

Smiling at herself for her quick thinking, she opened the door like she wasn't up to anything at all and breezed out into the hallway. Then flattened against the wall in the shadows as soon as she saw the one guard standing down there.

Okay, you have to get past that guy. He isn't going to let you go down to breakfast. He'll tell you to go back into your chamber and then he'll send someone up.

Panting a bit now in panic, she stuck to the side of the hallway and crept toward the intersection in the shadows. The man was pacing away from her. The stone floor wouldn't creak if she ran. Should she just run to the intersection and turn the corner before he turned around? Her feet were running before she even knew it. Around the corner the hall was larger, and there were alcoves she could hide in. She found it almost too easy to get to the stairs and go down both floors. When she cracked open the door at the bottom of the stairs into the great hall and saw that it was empty, elation took her over. She was going to do this. She was going to get away.

But then when she reached out to open the door, her hand wouldn't go.

What in the world?

Galdus's evil laughter echoed around her mind,

bouncing off her empty hopes and hitting her psyche. "Ye didna think it would be this easy, did ye?"

Furious, she reached for the door all the harder, straining to grab it and open it again.

But her hand wouldn't budge.

And now she felt herself turning around, albeit slowly and clumsily, toward the stairs that now reached up. She fought to turn back around toward the door, fought with all her might. But her body betrayed her, turning resolutely toward the stairs. And ascending both flights. Entering the large hallway.

Galdus tried to open Lauren's mouth. Tried to make her speak to the guard.

This, she absolutely refused to do, clamping her jaws, squeezing so they couldn't open. She would not speak her own doom.

Nevertheless, her traitorous body took her down the large hall, behind the guard, down the smaller hall, and right back into the chamber she'd been so happy to escape.

Chapter Fourteen

Hours later, Galdus had forced Lauren to unmake her rope so that her body had covers to keep it warm in the chill Scottish July air, but she didn't think she had slept a wink. She was still unable to control her movements. Galdus had a firm hold on most of her body, but he had not been successful at making her mouth form the words or utter the sound that would tell the guard where she was while she crept behind him in the outer hallway. She savored that victory, hoping it would give her the confidence she needed to go on.

At the same time, she knew his magic was much stronger than she was, and so she tried to reason with him.

"Galdus, let me just put ye doon here and leave. Ye wull see yer fellow druid friend when he returns just the same. Ye said it yerself, ye dinna need me."

But Galdus responded insistently.

"Nay, my love. I dae need ye, if only tae keep me out o' the hands o' Laird Donald. He covets my power like nae other I hae ever encountered, and though Taran has left ye now, Yer verra dear friend Jessica does still live close by, eh? I yet see the future where Donald wields me as verra bad for all the people ye hold dear tae yer heart."

Lauren tried to get up out of the bed, but it was useless. At least he hadn't made her undress. She thought she might die of mortification if she were lying naked here in the bed when Donald came back. Galdus had responded to reason, so reason she would continue to use.

"The longer I bide here, the greater the chance o' ye falling intae the hand o' Donald. Dae ye na see? We need tae leave now, while the going's good."

The first time, Galdus's chuckle was indulgent, the kind of laugh a man might have for his favorite niece, if she asked him for some small favor.

"Aw, Yer sense o' urgency is now quite keen, I see. All o' my urging ower this year has na went tae waste. More's the pity. The time for leaving is past. Dae ye na hear the jangle o' weaponry that comes with the footfalls on yon hard stone doon the hall?"

She got a sinking feeling in her stomach when she realized she did hear the approach of a warrior.

The door opened and Donald entered, looking winded and battle worn. like he'd ridden straight from the battle and come here without stopping to refresh. Several of his minions entered with him, all standing back at curt attention to await their laird's command. He and they were without a single drop of the camaraderie Leif shared with his men.

When Donald spoke, it was as if he were granting her a wish, he was so full of himself. "'Tis good tae come home tae see ye here, Lauren." He reached out his hand as if to help her up.

She cringed from him.

Instantly, Galdus made her roll over on the bed away from him and jump up on the other side.

For once, she agreed with the movement. In her weakened state of not having any sleep, she would be putty in his hands, lacking the strength to resist a grab for Galdus even with the druid dagger's help.

"Ye are welcome," Galdus intoned.

"I did na thank ye," She thought at him hard.

All she got was a chuckle.

Fortunately, Donald was amused and chuckled as well, once more looking her up and down with new appreciation, this time at her apparent quickness. She didn't care to think what the Laird o' the Isles would do if he were angry right now, with all these men in her chamber.

"Fiercely independent, ye are," said Donald. "I fancy that in a lass."

Bile rose in her throat at the idea of him liking her for anything other than her time travel knowledge. She didn't say anything, just stood there amid all these men and did as Galdus bade: held all her limbs as close to her body as she could.

"Good, my love," purred Galdus in her mind. "Make yerself as small a target as ye can. 'Twill be easier for me tae forge yer movements that make ye evade the Laird's grabs."

But the laird wasn't grabbing, and this worried Jessica more than if he had been. No, Donald's eyes were distant and hopeful, filled with schemes. Schemes that clearly involved her.

"Care tae follow me?" Donald called over his shoulder as he left the room very nonchalantly, as if she had a choice in whether to follow him or not. But all the other men stood there waiting for her to follow, and the looks on their faces told her she had better, or else.

Lauren tried not to go. She truly doubted they would harm her. She knew Galdus wouldn't let them —

"Dinna be sae certain o' that, lass. 'Tis true I will na let them strike ye doon intae death, howsoever ye can be in much pain and still keep me from falling intae Donald's hands. 'Twould serve ye wull tae remember that."

Sighing, she followed Donald down the small hall, around the corner into the larger hall, down both staircases, and into the great hall.

Donald strode straight to the throne and sat down. And then he looked at the throne by his side and raised his eyebrows. "I hae had a bit o' a change in my mind syne last we spoke, Lauren. My current thinking is that ye should become my wife. I will still remove the curse that is upon ye and relieve ye o' the object we spoke o', but I believe ye would be better off with me, and I with ye. With yer talents and my power, think o' all we could accomplish." He smiled as if he had offered her a vast fortune instead of a life of servitude. He relaxed in the throne as if it had been his since birth instead of the spoils of his aggressive campaign to take over all of Scotland.

"Accept his offer," Galdus said immediately, urging her to do just that by trying to exert control over her tongue. "This wull keep him pacified till my friend returns. 'Tis perfect. Accept his offer."

Lauren could see how it would be expedient to accept Donald. Galdus was right in that it would pacify the laird. But there was no way she was going to marry Donald, not him nor any she didn't want. A marriage of convenience was nothing she would ever settle for. And she took Galdus's meaning, about just what specific type of very intimate pacifying she would be doing.

Galdus tried to prevent her from refusing, but for whatever reason, she still maintained control of her speech, even though he was controlling her move-ments. "I am na interested in that offer, Donald. I decline."

She wasn't sure what she expected to happen next.

In any case, what did happen was anything but expected. It almost made her wish she had accepted him.

No, it didn't. Not even almost.

With a matter-of-fact look on his face, Donald got up from the throne and walked toward a different staircase, the one that went down into the dungeons. "It does na matter. We will get what we need from ye, one way or the other. Bring her."

Galdus was laughing his giddy evil laugh and making her follow Donald, so there was no reason for the men to put their hands on her, but they did anyway. Two grabbed one arm and two the other. They all but dragged her down the stairs and into a dungeon cell.

Galdus laughed a lot over the next few hours as they attempted to remove him and anything else from her person by brutal means that only a dungeon would have.

But Galdus was quickly in her hand, and she gave better than she got by a long shot.

Well, Galdus gave better than she got. Effortlessly and seamlessly, he moved her body in order to put himself between her person and everything they tried to do to her.

They tried to bind her.

Galdus moved her arms so that he cut through rope and chain alike!

They continued to hold her by the arms and tried to scar her with red-hot pokers.

Galdus cut and nicked and sliced their hands.

They tried to whip her.

Galdus cut up a dozen whips right out of thin air.

They pushed her into a dungeon cell and threw heavy stones at her.

Galdus made her catch the stones and throw them back, injuring two men and shattering one wooden cell door, along with severely bruising her hands.

They were installing a new door on her dungeon cell when finally, Donald called a halt. "This is na getting anywhere. The lass is injured and tired. We wull just leave her here. What we canna dae with force, we will allow Nature tae take care o'. Bring her naught, nae food, nae water."

Everyone left. Everyone except Galdus, and he was the one she really wanted gone.

She tried to get up, but his control and her exhaustion made it impossible. She would rest a bit and try again, because if she didn't get out, she was going to die here.

Chapter Fifteen

Battered and bruised, thirsty and exhausted, Lauren saw spots in the air, growing bigger and bigger. At the same time, she grew light-headed, her knees gave out, and she slumped surprisingly slowly down onto the cold stone floor.

The next thing she knew, she was in one of the strange bedrooms in the huge underground palace beneath Dunskey Castle. Every other time she'd shown up in Kelsey's dream version of her real-life jobsite, she'd been seated on one of the many thrones in the great hall, with Jessica and Katherine on thrones beside her. This time was much different. She was in the oddest bed. It was made of stone and shaped like a bowl, filled with handmade bedding. It was oddly comfortable, wide enough that most of her body lay on the bottom, but her legs and upper torso were propped up by the sides of the bowl. As she contorted her body to get to a standing position, she wondered why anyone would have such a strangely shaped bed and how they got out of them.

Kelsey's voice greeted her from across the room. "I think you should stay right there."

"Very funny," Lauren told one of her oldest friends from the Renaissance Faire, back in their teens. "I know you control this dream, so just get me out, already."

"Very well, but only because you asked so nicely."

The best thing about Kelsey's dream realm was that Galdus couldn't penetrate it. He wouldn't hear what went on and he couldn't influence what she said or did. This was Kelsey's personal dream realm, and Kelsey had complete control of it.

Just like that —the way it always is in dreams— Lauren was out of the bed and standing.

"So what are you doing asleep at this hour?" Kelsey asked with concern in her face. "I'm surprised to find you, but glad." With this last bit, Kelsey gave Lauren a quick hug and started to pull away.

Lauren clung to her friend,. "Tell me you can get me out of this mess, Kel. Galdus has gotten so he can control my movements. I can't do anything to resist him. He completely takes over my body and controls what I do. It's frightening. And that's not all."

As she spoke this next bit, she remembered it and

Kelsey made it part of the dream. It played like a holographic movie, all around them.

"Right now I'm in a dungeon locked in a cell inside a castle that's been taken over by the enemy, Donald MacDonald, Lord of the Isles. Leif and Taran fought him in a battle today, and I don't even know if they're alive — but the worst part is Taran thinks I've gone over to his enemy, Kel! I haven't of course. I was just trying to get on Donald's good side while I waited for Galdus's Druid friend Roland to return and take Galdus off my hands. I had to make nice so Donald wouldn't kill me. I also had to touch Taran to save his life, so now Galdus can hear his thoughts. For a brief time, Taran and I could hear each other's thoughts and it was wonderful! But Galdus ruined it all by not letting Taran hear my thoughts while I was stuck in a bedroom talking to Donald in the castle! Oh, and Katherine disappeared. I think she went to another time."

Kelsey hugged her fiercely. "Lauren, I will get you out of there. I will send help. Hold on, do you hear me? Hold on. I have to go so that I can get you out, but I will get you out, do you hear?"

"I hear you," Lauren whined, "I hear you, and in my mind I understand, but I don't want you to go. Can you take me with you? Are we going to somebody else's dream?"

Kelsey stroked Lauren's hair and held her face

tenderly against her own. "No, I'm not just going to someone else's dream. I have to wake up and go talk to somebody who can help us. His dreams are shielded, and he's not asleep right now."

Lauren soaked up all her friend's affection and comfort and then took a deep breath and let go of Kelsey. "Okay. Please, please, do what you need to. Just get me out of this dungeon cell. Donald has told everyone not to bring me any food or water. He's going to let me die of thirst."

Kelsey looked through Lauren for a moment and then her eyes widened in sympathy and shock. "Why didn't you tell me you were hurt? Before I go, there is one person we can bring into the dream to help you." She closed her eyes and concentrated for a moment, and then an older woman was with them, in the strange bedroom beneath Dunskey Castle. She had wise brown eyes and long curly gray hair. She was wearing a luscious green gown that looked all at once like emeralds and grass and the ocean. She raised her eyebrows in curiosity as she looked at Lauren, and then she too looked right through Lauren and gasped, taking hold of both of Lauren's hands and lightly pressing her forehead against Lauren's forehead. "Kelsey, you waited almost too long to get me. Be as still as you can, child. Still your thoughts and let me use all your energy for healing you."

Blissfully asleep and unaware of her body, Lauren didn't know if whatever the woman was doing was working or not. After a few moments the woman nodded at Kelsey and then vanished.

Lauren's friend hugged her again in the dream. "This can't wait, Lauren. I need to go right away, sorry. But you won't be alone long. Just hold on. One way or another, I will get you help."

Kelsey let go then and backed away. "Remember, I'm getting you help. You aren't alone. Just hold on. Got it?"

Lauren pulled herself together and nodded at her friend with confidence. "Thank you Kelsey I know you will help me. I can hold on."

Lauren had a few other dreams, the usual type. Talking to somebody she hadn't seen in years about why she'd bought a Mustang and not a Corvette. Trying to hang a pair of pants only to find they just would not go through the hanger but instead kept insisting on going over or under the hanger. Petting her dog she hadn't seen since she was a child.

And then at last it was time, and she woke up.

This time she knew exactly where she was when she opened her eyes. Her dungeon cell was small, maybe 8' x 5'. It held no bed and no bucket, nothing but herself. It was all made of stone except the wooden door, which had a tiny barred window that didn't close and only showed the stone of the deep dungeon hallway. Perhaps some prisoners were lucky enough to have food and water passed to them through this hole.

The best news was that her injuries were healed and she was no longer exhausted.

And then Lauren jumped at the sight of a face looking at her through the window.

Chapter Sixteen

Jessica was back in nursing school, only she couldn't find her patients. She kept running down long empty halls, desperate to find the people she was supposed to be caring for but not seeing them anywhere. All she found were empty beds which hadn't even been slept in. Regardless, she had devoted herself to caring for people. She had to keep looking.

Patients were waiting for her at the end of the hall, where the light was. She just knew it. But try as she might, she could never run fast enough to get there before the hallway extended and she was once again in the darkness. The hallway kept getting longer and longer and longer...

Wait. I'm dreaming, aren't I. This is one of my frustration dreams.

Knowing it was a frustration dream was most of the

battle, really. Over the years, she had figured out how to defeat them. If she stopped whatever she had been trying to do, it would turn into a normal fun dream. Sure enough, the hallways came to life with other nurses, doctors, technicians, and even patients walking around.

At the nursing station, Jessica saw Cecilia and Fran, some of her friends from back in college. They both smiled at her as if it was a big surprise that she was here with them.

"Where have you been?" Cecilia cried.

"Yeah," said Fran, "and where have you been working?"

Oh, it's just a dream. Let's have some fun with them.

Twirling her hair as if she were about to say some-thing embarrassing, Jessica looked up at the ceiling. "Well," she looked at them out of the corner of her eye and was amused to see them primed for juicy gossip, "Actually, I've time traveled back to the 1400s and am living as the lady of a manor house and am married to a gorgeous Scottish Laird." She looked at her friends again and was tickled pink at their reactions.

Fran and Cecelia were awestruck— mostly because the scene had shifted away from the hospital and they were now inside Cresh Manor, balking at all the hand-made details and the care that had been taken with every item in her home. Jessica was having great fun. However, she readily gave it up when Kelsey appeared and the scene became the damp but ornately carved stone corridors under Dunskey Castle.

Jessica ran to Lauren's longtime friend.

"Lauren's been kidnapped, Kelsey! Please tell me you can do something!"

Kelsey grabbed Jessica's upper arms and held on firmly but gently.

"I can do something, and I am doing something by visiting you. I've just been to see Lauren. It's not good. She's in a dungeon cell, and they're depriving her of water."

"How horrible!" Jessica said as she stared into Kelsey's face. "Please go help her! What are you doing here talking to me?"

Kelsey just looked at her with a piercing look in her eyes.

Jessica hadn't met Kelsey more than once briefly, so she didn't know the woman's facial expressions at all, yet... "I get the distinct impression you expect me to help Lauren."

Kelsey nodded!

Jessica scoffed. "That's ridiculous! How am I supposed to help her?"

§

TARAN WOKE UP WHILE THE SKY WAS STILL FILLED with stars. Needing to relieve himself, he walked a good distance away from where the other men were sleeping. He walked up the mountain, where he could have a view toward the castle where Lauren...

Nay, dinna think o' her.

He was shaking himself off when he saw movement down in the canyon between the two mountains. He wiped his hands with some wet leaves and then moved around some boulders to get a better look down into the canyon. He gasped. There were men moving down there, and they were moving away from the battlefield.

He ran to wake his brother.

"Leif. Leif! Awake, man," he yelled outside the low crevice under a large rock outcropping where Leif had lain down with Jessica the night before. Odd that she was na there now. Mayhap she had gone to relieve herself as well.

Leif opened his eyes, feeling about for his bride but not finding her.

Taran said in a hurry. "They're retreating toward the castle. Methinks 'tis Donald and his retinue!"

That brought Leif wide awake. He signed for Taran to back off, and as soon as Taran moved, Leif jumped up. When he gathered up his plaid to arrange it for walking instead of sleeping, he found in its folds a large piece of vellum, marked with writing.

He read it twice, uttering some choice words while he did. Sagging down, he put an arm against the rock outcropping. Resting his forehead on it for a moment, he handed the letter to Taran, who scanned it quickly the first time, then more slowly on the second read.

My dearest Leif,

By the time you read this, Kelsey will have summoned one of her colleagues, who will have spirited me away. Truly sorry I am to cause you worry, as I know this will.

Howsoever, someone needed to go and rescue Lauren. Before Kelsey came to me, she spoke with Lauren. She's in a dungeon cell in the castle, not in Donald's bedchamber as she was when Taran heard her before. Furthermore, Lauren suspects that Galdus was telling Taran lies about what was going on in the room. She was not enjoying Donald's company, just trying to get on his good side to protect herself.

Taran owes her a big apology for doubting her character.

As for how I plan to get Lauren out, I've been listening to your plans to go in through the tunnel. I'm confident that we can leave through them, once I get Lauren out of her dungeon cell.

If the tunnel exit is clear, then we shall make our way up over the mountain to Inverurie and will see you at home. Howsoever, if we see anyone when we look out the tunnel exit, then we will wait for you in the tunnel.

Yours till death do us part,

Jessica

Shame enveloped Taran, at how he had allowed himself to doubt Lauren. At how he had been there and should have tried harder to rescue her. But wallowing was for fools and drunkards. He fought off the shame. It was useless to him. Instead, he allowed anger at that deceiving Galdus to flood through him, giving him the strength he would need to storm the castle and get vengeance against Donald for having his men grab her away from him.

Their cursing had woken the men and drawn a crowd, but not so large a crowd as it might have been the morning before. They had left Inverurie with fifty men. Only twenty-nine remained able to fight. Six had been injured in the battle, and the rest were dead. Only eighteen of Ualraig's thirty knights who had joined them remained hale and hearty.

Taran bowed his head for a moment, saying a quick prayer for the dead and injured while he signaled for the gathered men to rouse anyone who still slept.

Once they were all assembled, Leif told them, "The Isles forces are retreating."

The men wore expressions of skepticism, but Leif bade them look to Taran.

"I did see it with my own eyes," he told them. "In the dark o' night, two score men flee tae Ualraig's castle. The rest o' the Isles dogs even now run for the hills toward their home in Islay."

A few had questions.

"Why would they leave?"

"For certies they canna be giving up sae easily?"

Another few discreetly pointed at the letter Taran had handed back to Leif, whispering quietly among themselves.

Leif ignored their whispers, holding up his hands for attention, which they quickly gave. Addressing Ualraig's remaining knights, he said, "More importantly, Donald thinks tae use yer laird's castle, as 'tis closer. I say we give him what he deserves. What say ye?"

"Aye!" yelled all the men, not just Ualraig's knights.

Leif raised his hands again, and this time he got silence right away. "We will recruit those we can from the local clans. Howsoever, let us na go near Alistair's camp. I will na disobey his orders, but neither will I be dissuaded from taking back what is oors."

All the men nodded their understanding.

Dawn was breaking when they reached the bloodied battlefield. Dead men lay everywhere by the hundreds, their faces aghast in defeat, their hands still clutching pikes and swords. Horses lay sprawled awkwardly as well. There were more dead from the Isles than from the local clans, perhaps three their two.

Taran looked this way and that to see if any wounded yet lay among the dead, but he saw only deathly white faces.

Those who were alive had camped right here on the battlefield, and Leif called out to those nearby as they passed, "We gae after Donald tae finish him! He has taken Ualraig's castle! Send whom ye can spare tae join us!"

The first camp he called to was the MacMurray clan's, and they didna take much time at all to decide who would go home to watch their lands and who would join the militia.

Next, a good half of Clan Irving's camp fell into the group with a shout.

"Gang forward!" yelled the Stirling clan when they heard the news.

Clan Leslie swelled their numbers.

And Clan Lovel.

The Maule clan joined in, as well.

The militia doubled its ranks, then tripled, and by the time they left the battlefield and headed up the first of two hills between them and the castle, the men were running.

Chapter Seventeen

When the militia was nearly to the top of the second hill, Leif signaled for a halt and signed for Taran to scout ahead and report back, indicating he would give Taran just enough time to steal his way to the trees and come back. If he didn't return within that time, they would come looking for him.

With a nod, Taran went off the path in order to conceal himself, climbed up the rest of the hill, and looked into the distance. He could see the gray stone towers of Ualraig's castle peeking up out of the trees. The towers were unmanned, and he didn't see anyone about. Using the local vegetation and rocks keep himself hidden from the road, he proceeded to the tree line, watching and listening for signs of people but not seeing or hearing anyone.

Taran had just turned around to use the road to

return to the militia when he heard Sky's voice behind him.

"They hae yer friend in the dungeon, that Lauren. I wull show ye where she is. Maybe ye can free the lass."

Taran was instantly suspicious and wary. The last time he saw Sky, he had been binding the man. Still, if he could show her right where Lauren was, that would be a help.

Acting as if he was tired — which he in no way was, but the lasses had told him exercise wasn't as plentiful in the future where Sky was from, and Sky didna pay much attention to anyone but himself — Taran sat down on the ground and surreptitiously stacked two three rocks in a manner that would signal the militia he was traveling to the castle with someone he had met on the way. "Just a moment. Let me catch my breath." Taran took a couple gasping breaths the way Lauren usually did after climbing the hill to the manor house, just to look convincing.

Apparently buying it, Sky stood there with his arms crossed, still moving his eyes with impatience. "She's yer friend, na mine. Take all the time ye will."

But if Taran took too long, the militia would come up over the hill looking for him. He preferred that Sky not know they were coming. "Verra wull, 'tis ready I am now. Lead the way."

Sky ran on ahead with a laugh, turning to look over his shoulder and make sure Taran was following. They ran for a few minutes until the castle was within sight between the trees.

Sky was leading Taran directly to the front gate. Did he think Taran was that slow in the head?

They had come far enough now that it wouldn't matter if Sky found out the militia was coming. They wouldn't be on the path to the castle gate now, but rather on their way to the entrance to the tunnels. If guards came along this path from the castle gate to investigate now, it would just mean there were fewer men inside the castle for the militia to fight.

Taran led Sky toward a nearby lookout hill. "I wull just signal Leif and the militia. I dinna think I wull be welcome at the front gate. Come with me."

Sky broke and ran for the castle gate, probably to warn them.

Taran stole through the brush and made his round-about way to the tunnel entrance.

Chapter Eighteen

L auren came out of being startled and took a
deep breath, then breathed easy, still staring
at the face she saw through the barred
window of her cell's new door.

"Jessica!"

Lauren's college roommate smiled in relief, no
doubt at finally being recognized. This brought back so
many memories, the strongest of which involved an
antique car Lauren and the other 39 fourth-year engineering students had disassembled one drunken
February night, down in a walled storage yard not far
from the engineering building.

She could still see every detail in her mind, as if it
had just happened yesterday. Lauren and Jessica were
filling her large rolling suitcase — which she of course
had lined with a spare bed sheet in order to protect it —
with hundreds of the car's smaller parts. Well, Lauren

was loading the parts into her suitcase by herself. But Jessica was keeping her company, standing up against the brick wall with her hands in her parka pockets, shivering as they talked.

The engineering students were reassembling the car in their main lecture hall as a senior prank, and there was a constant flow of students coming down here to grab parts and then turning around and running them to the building. Without fail, every last one of them was startled when they saw Jessica there and then addressed her as if she were a stranger who had wandered in there by accident.

"Can I help you find your way somewhere?"

Also without fail, Lauren told every last one of them the same thing.

"This is my roommate and best friend, Jessica. You've seen her a hundred times. She goes to all our parties, and she's always at the bar with us."

There was a jangling noise outside the newly hung dungeon cell door, and Jessica's face was turned downward so all Lauren could see was the top of her friend's head. The jangling stopped for a moment, then started again, stopped, started, and kept repeating that pattern for nearly five minutes.

Finally, the door flew open and Jessica rushed in, holding a ring of huge iron keys. "Surprise!" she said with a triumphant smile.

Lauren went to hug her friend. "Kelsey got you in here without any of the guards knowing?"

"Yep, but it was all done with her colleague's druid magic, so I don't have a great idea how we'll get out of the dungeon, but I figure we can use the tunnels the men are always talking about."

Lauren was about to say she thought she knew where they needed to go in order to get out through the tunnels, but she didn't get the chance.

Because horror overtook her.

Instead of going around Jessica's shoulder in order to deliver the hug Lauren intended, Lauren's right arm brought her hand down to draw the ancient jagged dagger out of its sheath!

"What are you doing, Galdus?"

Evil laughter was the only reply she got from the ancient evil druid.

But Galdus raised Lauren's other hand and used it to turn himself around so that her right hand held him like an ice pick. And his blade was pointing toward Jessica's chest!

Lauren could see her hand going toward Jessica's heart as if in slow motion, could tell it would be a fatal thrust.

It all happened so fast that Jessica hadn't even registered yet that she was in danger. She was still smiling at Lauren and reaching out to hug her.

"Run, Jessica!" Lauren squeezed out through her resistant lips.

Her friend's face ever so slowly changed from delight at seeing Lauren to horror at seeing Galdus come toward her. She dropped the keys and started to turn so she could run.

But not fast enough.

It took everything Lauren had — and if she hadn't been healed she knew she wouldn't have had it in her to stop Galdus from plunging into Jessica's chest. She couldn't stop the motion entirely. Her fist still swung out toward her friend. But Lauren was able to turn Galdus toward the wall.

Instead of stabbing Jessica in the heart, Lauren socked her in the chest.

The keys finished falling from Jessica's hand and hit the cold stone floor with a clatter.

The force Galdus had put into Lauren's thrust drove Jessica backward into the stone wall, where she bumped her head and then bounced onto the floor.

Even though she had managed to turn aside a fatal stab, Lauren was wracked with guilt about having hurt her.

"Jessica!" Lauren cried out, "Jessica, I'm so sorry. Please know it was Galdus who did it, not me. Jessica?"

Her friend wasn't responding. She lay motionless and unaware.

Lauren tried to run to Jess and help her, but the fight wasn't over. Lauren could feel Galdus gathering her arm for a downward thrust.

But this time, Lauren stopped him. "No. I am na gaun'ae stab my friend. Ye can dae anything ye want tae me, but ye are na gaun'ae make me harm my friend any more than ye already hae. I wish I had never laid eyes on ye."

Galdus's evil chuckle sought to take over her mind, filling every nook and cranny with its jarring staccato noise even as the urge to plunge the dagger down into Jessica's helpless form filled her arm, only relenting when he spoke. "Och, ye wull resist, but in the end, ye wull dae what I want ye tae. Ye ken ye wull."

"Nay, I willna."

Lauren fastened her eyes on the dagger. Concentrating on every motion she made, she forced her arm to lower the blade slowly. Forced her hands to turn it around in her grip. Forced herself to sheath the thing and let it go.

She didn't have time to breathe the heavy sigh of relief she wanted breathe, though. Instead, she prayed to God that Jessica was all right as she gently took her friend's pulse. At first she didn't feel anything, and despair so heavy she could barely breathe overtook her. But there it was. A faint heartbeat. And then another. Sighing that sigh of relief at last, she picked Jessica up in a fireman's hold by throwing her friend's arm over her shoulder and then standing. Fortunately, Jessica wasn't very heavy.

She thought she knew the way out through the tunnels. She had a pretty good idea, and she knew at least she had to go this way —

But as soon as Lauren stepped into the hallway

with her burden, she found herself blocked by two of Donald's guards.

&.

TARAN DIDN'T SEE THE LASSES WHEN HE ENTERED the tunnels, but he heard Jessica's voice calling out Lauren's name in a frightened tone.

"Lauren! Put me down!"

He didn't think, just sprang into action, shimmying through the tight twisted series of hallways that hid the tunnel from inside and into the dungeon.

Running down the hall toward the voices, he put his back up against the wall when he got to the third intersection and saw one of Donald's guards. Taran didn't have time to wait for the man to go relieve himself or something. So he rushed him. The encounter reassured Taran that Donald and his men still didn't know about the tunnel, because he caught the man by surprise and was able to knock him out before he was any the wiser.

Jessica's voice had come from a place whose sound he remembered from playing hiding games down here with the other children the one time he visited in his youth. Before he even thought about it, he was running down this new corridor.

He slowed when he heard Donald's voice, and he stopped at the last intersection, crouching down so that when he peered around the corner, he wouldn't be where anyone would be looking for a face to appear..

Donald was moving toward Lauren with his sword drawn.

A low growl escaped Taran's throat as he jumped up and charged toward Donald. But he felt a slam from behind and went down on the cold stone floor. He struggled with his attacker, but the man was unbelievably strong. Unnaturally strong. A druid must have magicked him.

At long last rolling onto his back and catching a glimpse of his attacker, who was holding him down easily, Taran gasped.

Sky smiled at him, a cruel superior smile, before looking over toward Donald. "Laird, I hae brought ye a gift."

Chapter Nineteen

Taking advantage of Donald's distraction, Lauren made sure to keep Jessica behind her while she looked over toward Sky's voice. She needed to see if the gift he had brought was dangerous. Her gaze flew over the two guards and the empty stone passageway to her right and landed on the man in flowing tie-dyed robes. Who had Taran in a headlock.

Her heart raced, and though she knew it was foolish, she screamed, "No!"

Sky's eyes slithered up and down her trembling body while he dragged Taran over so that he was standing right next to her, holding her man helpless and saying to her breathlessly, "Oh yes."

Taran's face was still fierce with determination, but when his eyes met hers they softened for an instant, then pleaded with her for forgiveness.

She gave him her anguished face, to show him he needn't worry about her love for him. But even though she could feel the ancient druid's presence in her mind, she would not beg him to let her and Taran hear each other's thoughts. She would never ask him for anything ever again. She was done communicating with Galdus.

Donald nodded at Sky in appreciation but turned his sickening smile on Lauren while he spoke to the man. "I thank ye for the gift. Howsoever, it must needs bide awhile. This lass has some aught I want, and I hae come tae believe the only way I wull get it is tae kill her."

Lauren's mouth went dry at the threat, but she kept her head. She had one chance. Time enough for one action before Donald dropped his fake charm and attacked her with his sword, which would doubtless cause Galdus to try even harder to exert control over her...

She knew what the best course of action was. Fighting against Galdus with her newfound willpower born of remorse, Lauren drew him from his sheath. Readied him.

And she stabbed the dagger into Sky's side, making the hippie scream in pain.

And more to the point, making him release Taran.

Unarmed but far from defenseless, Taran wasted no time in rushing out of Sky's grasp to put himself between her and Donald.

But Sky pulled the blood-dripping dagger out of

his side and turned on the Laird o' the Isles. With a maniacal laugh that had to be coming from Galdus, he rushed the laird, slicing and dicing through the air like a ninja. Galdus was more than a match for Donald's skill, Lauren knew from experience having Galdus help her fight.

It was like a train wreck. Lauren felt herself transfixed, standing there watching Sky attack Donald.

But Taran had more sense. He grabbed both her hand and Jessica's and started running back the way he'd come in. The three of them ran through the tunnels toward the exit, Lauren lighting their way with a torch she had managed to grab from a wall sconce.

Taran's hand felt so good in Lauren's, sending into her very core the reassurance that all would be right from now on. There was no more tension between them. They just needed to get back to Leif and everyone, back home.

"Not much farther," said Taran, seeming to read her mind even though they had no chance of ever again hearing each other's thoughts, now that Galdus was gone. Good riddance to bad rubbish!

Lauren was nearly jerked off her feet. Taran righted himself immediately, though. What could have caused him to stumble?

Lauren glanced over and saw that Jessica, unaccustomed to fieldwork and frankly more active this past year than she'd been in all the years Lauren had known her, had tripped over a guard who lay prone on the cold stone floor of the cave-like dungeon.

"Look where you're going!" Lauren chided her friend with a wry grin.

"I guess so," Jessica quipped. "After all, bodies on the floor are to be expected, when running through a dungeon."

"Hush, lasses," Taran scolded. But he was also laughing a bit.

After that their run grew easier for a time, but then Jessica moaned. "I hae a stich in me side. Pray slow!"

But Taran just scooped Jessica up in a fireman's carry, throwing her over his shoulder and then grabbing Lauren's hand again to keep running.

After a while they heard sounds of pursuit behind them, and Lauren did her best to run faster.

And then they rounded a corner and met up with Leif and the militia, who were tense at first sight but visibly relaxed when they saw it was them coming and not some of Donald's men. Several militiamen stepped toward them to use Lauren's torch to light torches they had made.

Once she was back on her feet, Jessica ran into Leif's arms. The two embraced.

Taran pulled on Lauren's hand until she gently swung into him, and he helped her hold the torch above them while he grabbed her up in an embrace as well. It was heavenly. She clung to him, willing him to understand just how much... But by all he had done this past half hour, not to mention the warmth and ardor of his kiss, she could tell he did. Nothing needed to be said.

Leif and Taran then turned around to face their pursuers, both signaling, "Jessica, Lauren, go behind everyone, but stay with us so we can protect you."

Lauren saw the same relief she felt mirrored in her friend's face. Safe and protected once more, they ran to the back of the militia, where Jared nodded and smiled at them before turning around, gesturing for them to stay right behind him, which they gladly did as the militia jogged forward.

It didn't take long for their pursuers to catch up to the militia, a force to be reckoned with. The militia knew their way around, while these close quarters were still unfamiliar to Donald's men. They were on their way in two minutes.

Lauren noticed bodies on the floor once they were all through, but the militia started jogging, and she rushed to keep up. They met more guards and dealt with everyone they met until they were at the top level of the dungeons near the stairs that went up into the castle proper.

All communications in the militia were silent warrior gestures, but Lauren and Jessica had played Charades with the men often and followed the conversation easily.

Leif did most of the communicating.

"We have the advantage down here. We know the

lower tunnels well, and they weren't even aware of them. We'll go back down there. Lure the few guards who are left down here toward us..."

Lauren raised her eyebrows and smiled at Jessica, who did the same back.

It was a good plan.

So the militia turned around and soon they were jogging back the other way, this time with Lauren and Jessica in front of them. They went down one more level into the area where Taran hadn't encountered any more guards because Donald didn't know the tunnel went all the way out. This last bit was hidden cleverly behind two turns of a corner that was very narrow, easy to miss if you didn't know it was there.

"Jared," Leif pointed, "go up and draw one of the guards down here."

Jared thumped his fist on his heart and ran back up the tunnels.

Without thinking about it, Lauren went over to Taran's side and clung to him while they waited. He clung back and pulled her into another embrace, resting his head on top of hers and cupping the back of her head gently with his hand as he rocked back-and-forth. And then he quickly pulled away and gently pushed her behind him when they heard footsteps running toward them in the hallway.

Holding all their torches, five of the militiaman ran toward Jared and the guard.

When the guard saw them, he turned around and ran the other way.

They let him go.

The militia then advanced down the tunnel a ways, again with Lauren and Jessica behind them. They stayed within the part that was unfamiliar to Donald's men. They didn't have to wait long. Twenty men came to deal with the five they thought awaited them, and those men were dispatched quickly by the militia.

Keeping Lauren and Jessica with them but in the back, the militia swept through the dungeons, up the stairs, and throughout the castle. But they discovered that Donald had left and only a few men remained. Rather than kill the men who had surrendered, they told them to leave and not come back. They held the castle.

Lauren looked all over, but there was no sign of Sky and Galdus.

Chapter Twenty

U alraig was nowhere to be found. They presumed him dead, but over the next few days, his wife and children came back from where they'd been hiding in the mountains, along with all the other wives and children.

Donald and his men had drunk most of the whiskey and eaten through most of the stores, but there was time yet before winter. They would be all right.

The militia went home to Inverurie, and Leif, Jessica, Taran, and Lauren went home to Cresh Manor.

Amena ran out to greet them, throwing herself around first Leif's leg and then Taran's as she cried and laughed at the same time with joy at her brothers being home.

Senga stood back wringing her hands, but first Leif went over and hugged her and then Taran did as well.

She turned her sad eyes on them. "Sae Luag and Katherine perished in the battle?"

Leif turned puzzled eyes on Senga, shaking his head. "We dinna ken."

But Lauren spoke up. "No, they went time traveling. I suspect Katherine took Luag home to our time."

Leif sighed. "Here's hoping they return soon. The Druids hae na acted, and I suspect the worst is yet tae come. We need all the help we can get."

Everyone nodded in agreement, even little Amena.

"Dinna fash," Jessica told her husband. "Katherine does na ken she wants Luag with her, and sae she will dae all she can tae send him away. I would na be surprised if Luag popped back among us this verra instant."

They all had a good laugh at that.

Lauren watched Taran saunter over to where his brother stood with his bride. She had a feeling she knew what he was going to say.

She was right.

"There will be battles with us always," said Taran, "'tis a fact o' life. We canna cast living aside. We must take joy where we can find it, or be doomed tae constant sorrow. Sae, Laird Leif, can ye see yer way tae allowing Lauren and I tae hae Gammer's cottage? We will be needing a bit o' privacy, at least for a year or sae."

This made the adults laugh. Amena just looked at

them all with a question in her eyes, which none of them answered.

Leif smiled first at Taran and then over at Lauren, squeezing Jessica's hand. Jessica smiled at them both too, with a wink for Lauren.

"Aye," said Leif, "Ye can hae Gammer's cottage, but not afore we go disturb Father Craig's supper again."

Afterword

Don't worry, Luag and Katherine do return to 1411 soon. Once back, they use their considerable powers of persuasion to help our friends stave off a continuing war fueled by the druids.

Luag's time stuck in the modern world is just the first few chapters of Katherine and Luag's romance story.

Here's a picture of Taran as Santa, because it exists!

Also by Jane Stain

Tavish

Seumas

Tomas

Kilts at the Renaissance Faire

Time of the Celts

Time of the Picts

Time of the Druids

Leif

Taran

Luag

All my Jane Stain books are exclusively available on Amazon.

Sign up for new book alerts at www.janestain.com

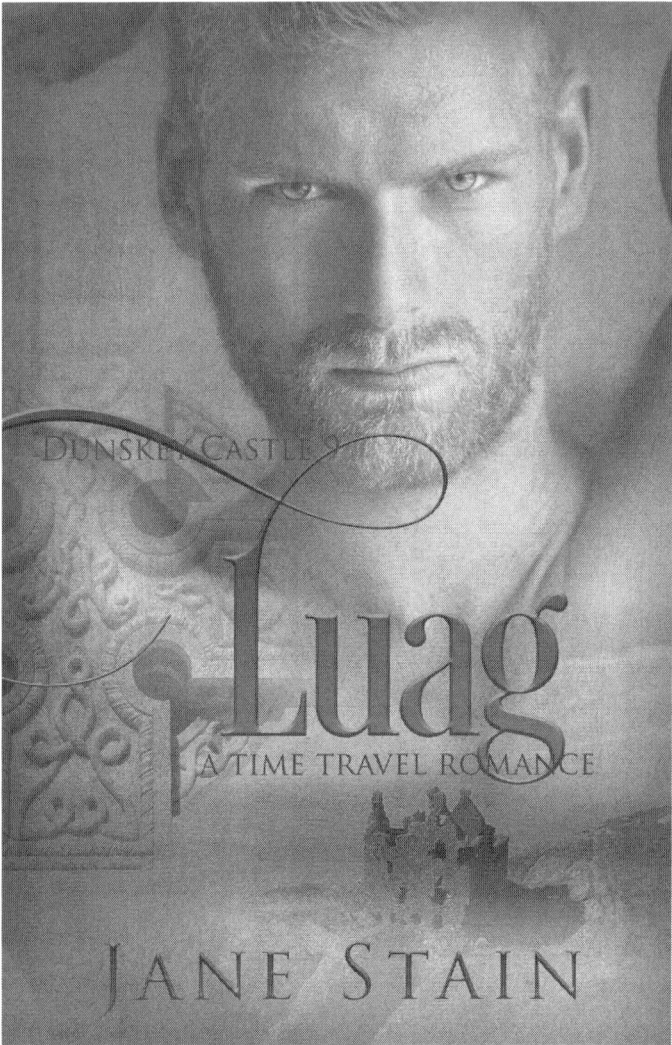

DUNSKEY CASTLE

Luag

A TIME TRAVEL ROMANCE

JANE STAIN

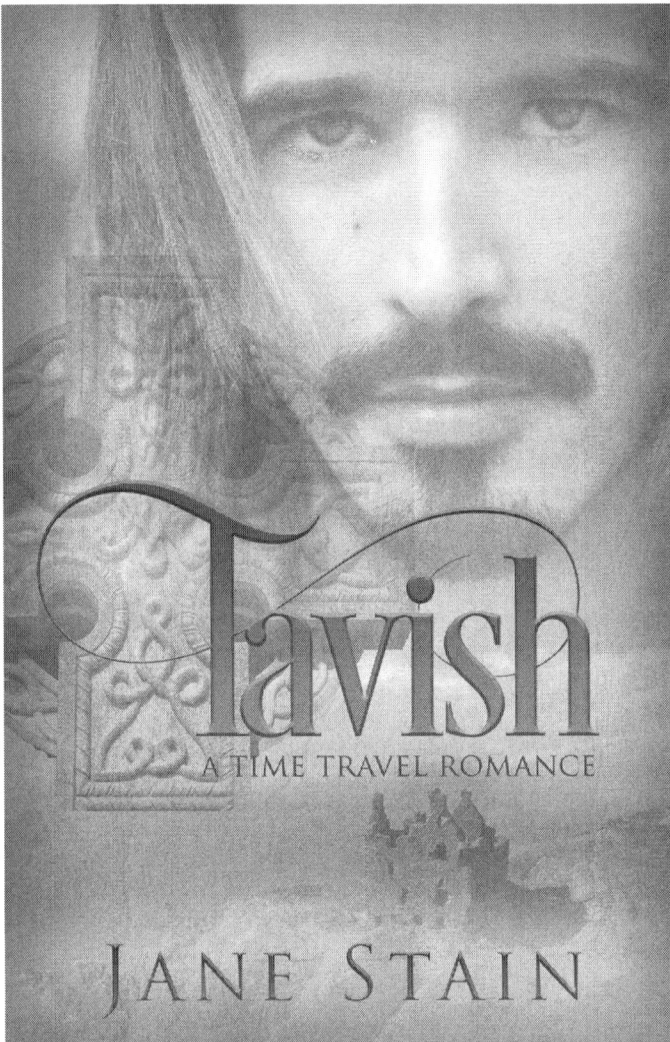

Tavish

A TIME TRAVEL ROMANCE

JANE STAIN

Dunskey Castle 2

Seumas

A TIME TRAVEL ROMANCE

JANE STAIN

DUNSKEY CASTLE 3

Tomas

A TIME TRAVEL ROMANCE

JANE STAIN

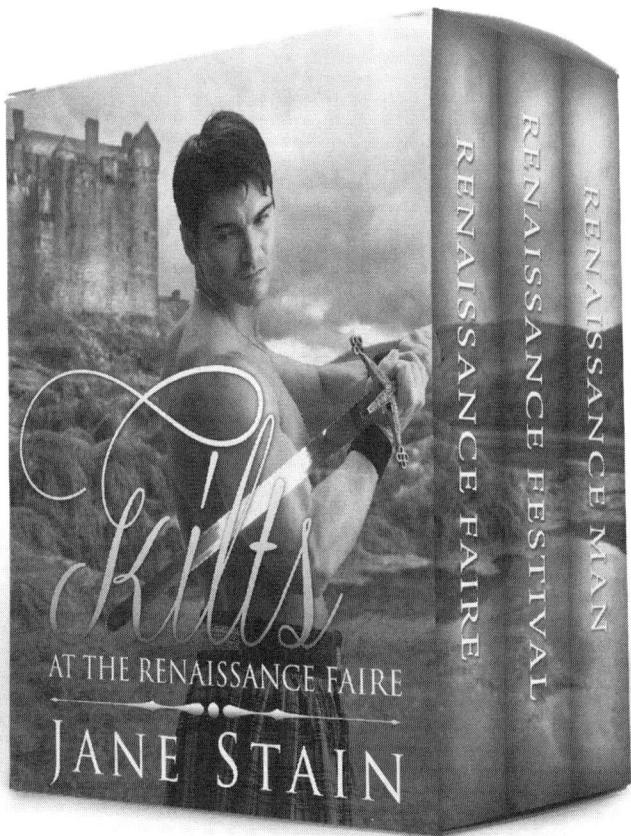

Kilts
AT THE RENAISSANCE FAIRE

JANE STAIN

RENAISSANCE FAIRE

RENAISSANCE FESTIVAL

RENAISSANCE MAN

Dunskey Castle 4

Time of the

Celts

A Time Travel Romance

JANE STAIN

DUNSKEY CASTLE 5

TIME OF THE

Picts

A TIME TRAVEL ROMANCE

JANE STAIN

Time of the
Druids

A time travel romance

Jane Stain

DUNSKEY CASTLE 7

Leif

A TIME TRAVEL ROMANCE

JANE STAIN

As Cherise Kelley

Dog Aliens 1: Raffle's Name

ISBN: 1480063592

Dog Aliens 2: Oreo

ISBN: 1481923013

Dog Aliens 3: She Wolf Neya

ISBN: 1481923374

——

My Dog Understands English!

ISBN: 1494263807

High School Substitute Teacher's Guide

ISBN: 1479229644

All my Cherise Kelley books can be ordered wherever you buy paperbacks online. Stores don't stock them on the shelves, but they can order them for you.

Bookstores will want the ISBN when ordering.

About the Author

Jane Stain is a pen name. My real name is Cherise Kelley. I was born in 1963.

My mother put herself through nursing school when I was 10-13 years old. I helped her study for her exams, and my younger sister and I learned about tapeworms at the dinner table.

I have been married since 1994, but I dated two engineers before I met my husband.

I acted and sang from 1988 - 1992 at the Renaissance Pleasure Faire. This is the very first renaissance fair. Founder Phyllis Patterson invented the idea.

Thank you for reading all this. If you have read this far, then you must have enjoyed something about Taran and Lauren's story. I hope you will post a customer review on Taran's Amazon page and tell other readers what that was.

Just Google "Jane Stain Taran". I will read it too. :)

San Luis Obispo Renaissance Fair in 1990.
Me with Dan Willens and Jeanette Moorehead
in our improvisational play: "Wheel of Fairy
Tales"

Me at Stonehenge in 1989 on Shortest Day, one of
two days a year the landowner lets people near the
stones. Thanks again for my graduation present, Mom!

Made in the USA
Columbia, SC
07 November 2021

48476248R00124